PULP *Literature*

PULP LITERATURE PRESS

Issue No. 37, Winter 2023

Publisher: Pulp Literature Press; Managing Editor: Jennifer Landels; Senior Editor: Mel Anastasiou; Acquisitions Editor: Genevieve Wynand; Poetry Editors: Daniel Cowper & Emily Osborne; Assistant Editors: Brooklynn Hook, Nik Kos, Melisa Gruger, Jeya Thiessen, Sierra Louie, Ellen Sapcey; Copy Editor: Amanda Bidnall; Proofreaders: Mary Rykov, Sierra Louie; Graphic Design: Amanda Bidnall; Cover Design: Kate Landels; Subscriptions: Carol McCauley; Advertising: Brooklynn Hook. For advertising rates, direct inquiries to info@pulpliterature.com.

Cover painting, *Erebus and Terror at Beechey Island* by Kristina Gehrmann. Artwork for 'A Cold Place Between the Shores' by Artyom Trakhanov. All other illustrations by Mel Anastasiou.

Pulp Literature: ISSN 2292-2164 (Print), ISSN 2292-2172 (Digital), Issue No. 37, Winter 2023.

Published quarterly by Pulp Literature Press, 21955 16 Ave, Langley, BC, Canada V2Z 1K5, pulpliterature.com, at $15.00 per copy. Annual subscription $50.00 in Canada, $72.00 in continental USA, $86.00 elsewhere. Printed in Victoria, BC, Canada, by First Choice Books / Victoria Bindery. Copyright © 2022 Pulp Literature Press. All stories and works of art copyright © 2022 their authors as per bylines.

Pulp Literature Press gratefully acknowledges the support of the Canada Council for the Arts.

Pulp Literature is a proud member of the Magazine Association of BC and Magazines Canada.

TABLE OF CONTENTS

FROM THE PULP LIT PULPIT

On Time

Whether by default or design, publishing a quarterly magazine is necessarily seasonal. And four times a year, at write-the-editorial time, the current season is on proud display just outside my window. Meanwhile, the publication date of this issue beckons me forward to the next.

As seems to be the case for many publishers these days, those duelling seasons are not only beginning to nuzzle against one another but are, in fact, becoming aligned. As I write this, there's snow on the ground, and ice on the sidewalks, and a fire in the fireplace. It is entirely possible that you, dear reader, are holding this, our winter issue, while spring's first buds begin to bloom.

Yes, we could cite the pandemic or paper shortages or printing delays, but, really, it no longer matters. Quite simply, we are glad to be with you now. The stories and poems and art with which we have spent many months are here, and they are yours. We are delighted to meet you in this shared space, where all things become possible.

Speaking of the four seasons, within this issue, we've

got a few more: there's tax season and bear season and the holiday season. There's a season each for magic and muscles and superheroes. And our feature story reminds us that, in the wake of climate change, there remain unknown seasons yet to come.

As writers and readers know, stories don't just have their own meaning. Like seasons, they have their own momentum. We're so glad you are along for the ride.

~*Genevieve Wynand*

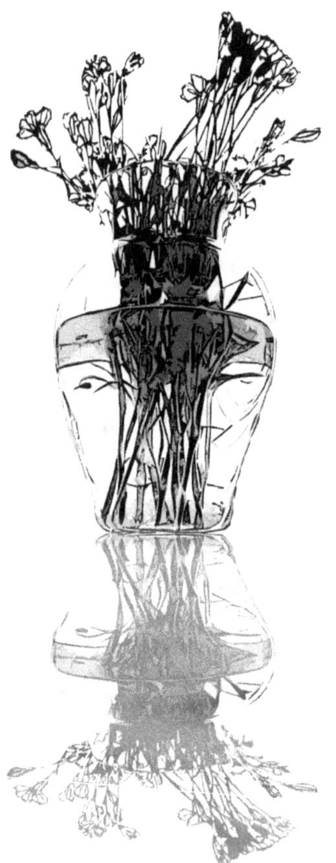

In THIS ISSUE

Our stunning cover, *Erebus and Terror at Beechey Island* by **Kristina Gehrmann**, may depict the ill-fated Franklin expedition, but your journey through our pages will be smooth sailing …

Feature author **Renée Sarojini Saklikar** weaves poetry and prose in 'Told under the Linden Tree', to tell a new tale from her epic saga *THOT J BAP*. And it's a matter of do or fly for superheroes of a different stripe in 'Falling for You' by **Tom Jolly**.

Bears offer the promise of transformation and redemption in 'Slip into My Fur' by **Patrick Barb**, Hummingbird

Flash Fiction winner 'Not What You Think' by **Alan Sincic**, and 'A Cold Place Between the Shores' by **Mikael Lopez** and **Artyom Trakhanov**.

Flex, fight, and fetch with flash fiction in **Finnian Burnett**'s 'Ethan Peck's Muscles' and 'Nothing Left' and **MJ Malleck**'s 'The Dog I Loved'.

Check the fit of a different life in 'Regarding Line 25600 of Your Income Tax Return' by **Cadence Mandybura** and 'Zara's Song' by **JM Landels**.

The flame of lost love burns in the final instalment of *Pretty Lies* by **Mel Anastasiou**, while family takes centre stage in poetry by **Catherine Lewis** and **Jude Neale**.

TOLD UNDER THE LINDEN TREE

Renée Sarojini Saklikar

Renée Sarojini Saklikar (*Surrey Poet Laureate, 2015–2018*) *is the author of four books and six chapbooks. Her work has been adapted for opera and visual art. She teaches creative writing and has judged our Magpie Award for Poetry. Renée's sci-fi epic in verse,* Bramah and the Beggar Boy, *was published in 2021, and her new book,* Bramah's Quest, *is forthcoming spring 2023 from Nightwood Editions. Her short story 'Man with Golden Helmet' appeared in* Pulp Literature *Issue 28.*

Told under the Linden Tree

Migrant Camp #3
Outside Perimeter

Resisters from the Fifth Catastrophe,
we sit cramped in this holding cell:
no pencils, no scribes. Story forbidden.
Above us, wireless drones hover, darting
circles to watch, to catch, intent to learn
how we might transmit —

\>\>\>\>\>\>\>

A Winter's Tale: Waiting for Bramah

Our story starts in a valley beneath the icefields of an ancient mountain, snow cap metres deep, stable for aeons, and now shrinking epoch to decade, decade to year, year to month, centimetre or inch — either way, a winter regime of snow-drought, dry as dust.

One night, in a small shack, we huddled close, hands to a tin drum filled with the dying embers of coal and timber, remnants of the Before-Time. We shared stories and each story emitted a sonar-pulse reverberating upward to our thinning atmosphere. We knew somehow, someway, Bramah the Locksmith would hear us.

"Come, Bramah," we chanted in our circle. "Help us find the Portal of the Four Seasons," where once we knew temperate and not extreme.

"Bramah, bring your pick and your drill," we knew to add, for at the gate of the portal, the *Vault of the Lost*: in its chambers, a hundred thousand names of all the plants and animals, extinct. We'd saved what seeds we could.

An icy north wind rattled the walls of our shack, a shutter banged loose. Our story, paused. Was there another sound, perhaps a knock on wood? When we opened the door, there stood on the threshold three seed savers, arrived from foreign lands, cloaks bedraggled, burlap pouches covered against the snow.

"Crust, mantle, core," they whispered.

"To the bellows and for the warmth," we replied, our gaze intent on their expectant faces.

Of course, we offered what we could: dry *naan* bread and stale water from our well, the water table low as it had ever been. Together, we sat with the strangers.

They shared news from the east. None of it good. How that wind howled! We turned then, as before, to story and chants, to warm our cold bodies, to fill our near-empty bellies. We fanned the air with scented tales redolent with memory, where once we sat under the bloom of the Linden Tree. Each syllable spoken, sent out to the night stars, "Come, Bramah!"

We remembered old spells long forgotten, faint whisperings of wind rough against stone,

hollyhocks, daisies, snapdragons, and peas
we'll follow Albert the Mendicant, please
hollyhocks, daisies, snapdragons, and peas
hearts and bees dancing down to the Valley
Linden to Banyan come walk with us now——

The wind died down at dawn. Before our guests resumed their journey westward, they bent close to fragments of old texts tacked up inside our walls. Their fingers traced the paper. We nodded to see them read. Then they took their silent leave, save for two requests: one, that we would add to the walls of our shack notes about their arrival and departure, as a record for those who might come this way again. And two, when the next seed savers arrived, we'd again share our stories. And, so, here you are: shall we begin?

Ciswen the Blacksmith & Albert the Mendicant

Three days past summer solstice. Noon, and the sun burning down, the green grass fast turning brown. In the Before-Time, we'd click, tap, to check the times of sunrise to sunset, fractions misplaced with the Shift-Tilt. Now, we paced our morning steps to the sun, following bee dances, to stand under green boughs, to watch Ciswen the Blacksmith: tall, broad shouldered, forearms strong, white-blonde hair tied back in two long braids. Her eyes glowed cornflower blue when she worked at her forge; or, when irritated, narrowed to flint grey, her mouth set in two firm lines. At the sound of our footsteps, Ciswen grunted. Without lifting her head, her voice came at us, "Ah, my friends, you've returned, here with me again." We edged in closer to her workspace under the Linden Tree. Suddenly, a voice cried out, "Ciswen, Ciswen, don't start anything without me!" We all turned to see Albert the Mendicant loping towards us.

Ciswen glared at Albert. We said nothing.

"Now, Ciswen," said the mendicant. He held up a torn Before-Time paperback, as if to barter, three-quarters of a translation—*The Sand Reckoner*—Greek to Latin to English.

"Honestly, I've got nothing for you," said Ciswen.

"Not even the time of Bramah's arrival?" said the mendicant. "Not even a tale of skill and bravery?"

"Especially not that," said Ciswen. She mopped her glistening brow. We heard her add, under her breath, "You're always grubbing for stories." Albert thought, *Today, this very afternoon, I'll best her. Ponderous, cantankerous. But what skill her hands at the forge!*

Bees darted to suck pollen from the tiny flowers of the Linden Tree. Ciswen reached up to the lower boughs. Albert's gaze followed the length of her arm, then turned away. Albert didn't notice, as we did, how Ciswen caressed each leaf and flower. She let her hand fall to her side and sighed. Albert, eager to divine her thoughts, said, with exaggerated jollity, "Remember, last winter, how the ice on the lake never froze?"

Ciswen glared at Albert.

"Remember," said Albert, "the boughs of this very tree hung free from snow, and you told the most amazing story of the Before-Time and—"

Ciswen squinted at Albert, and he started to cough, gulping for air.

Albert looked up at the tree. Albert thought about the time he saw Ciswen swing a sledgehammer two-handed. She could beat iron, steel, bronze, fast and sure, deft with tongs, her huge hands measured and slow.

Things Albert Contemplated Saying to Ciswen but Did Not: "Tell me about your first meeting with Bramah."

"Tell me the secret of how you forged Bramah's titanium pick and drill."

"Tell me about your hair, each plait as blonde as ever was, since before the time of the Five Catastrophes."

"Also, now that I think of it, tell me, too, about Bramah's hair, sleek and black as ever we first saw her — since before the Great Abandonment. The years pass and yet you both look the same."

Instead of saying any of these thoughts, Albert made a great show of writing out a list of herbs he meant to acquire at his next stop in the valley, past Aunty Agatha's farm.

As Albert wrote his list, Ciswen closed her eyes, blew her forge fire low, and stood to rest against the mighty trunk of the Linden Tree.

Once, Ciswen remembered, a very long time ago, Albert had managed a hobby farm and raised llamas and goats. Ciswen forced herself not to laugh and recalled things she'd heard about Albert. He was untrustworthy, a spy for Perimeter and maker of unreliable potions. He price-gouged for things in demand.

Ciswen feigned sleep, willing Albert to leave.

But Albert, unreliable as he was, was also crafty. He didn't leave. He just plunked himself down under the Linden Tree, shifted closer to us, and waited. There we all sat on that hot summer afternoon. Bees buzzed amid the heavy scent of the

Linden Tree flowers. We all knew to wait for story. We all knew that sooner or later, Ciswen would begin — and she did; only, just as Ciswen launched into a story about Bramah's last visit to the valley, who should call out to us but two washerwomen, the sisters, Elm and Stone, on their way to the river.

"Hey, Ciswen, save us some mead," cried the sisters.

Ciswen opened her eyes and stared at them.

Elm and Stone were known far and wide as gossips, although everyone swore they made the best soap. And soap, along with storytelling, we don't need to remind you, is a boon for the times in which we live. Ciswen, with one shrug of her huge shoulders, affronted by interruptions, went back to working at her bench. Albert the Mendicant looked sideways at Elm and Stone. Everyone settled back under the Linden Tree. We watched Ciswen work: beat, pound, grunt, sweat. Elm and Stone smiled and said, "Ciswen, tell us about Magda the Wise, and didn't she make your fine leather apron envied by all the blacksmiths in Hidden Valley?"

Albert sat as quiet as a mouse and waited for Ciswen's reply. She didn't say anything. Well, not at first. Albert waited to see if anyone else might pass by the Linden Tree.

Our Observations of Albert the Mendicant and His Awkward Ways

Albert licked his dry lips. How he longed to ask Ciswen for a sip of mead. Instead, he looked down at the grass, and from the folds of his cloak pulled out his small notebook and pencil. *Words are snakes,* thought Albert. He determined that one day he would find and crush every word-snake in his path. When a skylark called, Albert looked up, not at the bird, but at his cart, parked at the edge of the meadow. Albert's cart, painted red and white, sat pleased with itself, packed high with boxes and sacks. In each box waited trays of vials, tiny glass bottles: tinctures and ointments, dried herbs. In each sack: silk scarves, pieces of old cotton batting, fragments of parchment.

I always save for a rainy day. Albert would laugh when he said this to the seed savers in Hidden Valley. Everyone bartered.

Sometimes children would follow behind Albert's cart and chant,

"mandrake or sea holly,
Albert you're all folly,
cardamom and ginger
we'll give you the finger,
   grey feathering wormwood
   put us to sleep or we'll fly
off on henbane,
   buzzed with turmeric,
bless us with rosemary,
peony to banish
   our bad dreams."

Albert, trusted by none, was always writing things down. When he took out his pencil — "My most valuable commodity," he told prospective customers — everyone got their backs up, arms folded across their chests. They stayed silent and pointed to his wares. Albert never rushed to make a sale. The longer the transaction, the more likely he could eavesdrop on a shared story. His fingers itched to write in words all the village gossip. If he wrote things down, he remembered better. If he remembered, he could repeat what he heard, wending up and down the valley. People tended to buy more if distracted by story, Albert observed. He'd also noticed the opposite: sometimes fingers poised to purchase somehow found their way back into pockets.

Maybe stories make them nervous, mused Albert. He thought about the last time he'd passed by the Linden Tree.

Albert the Mendicant Remembers the Way Elm and Stone Got a Story Out of Ciswen

Elm and Stone returned from up the river, bundles of clothes tied up with twine. These they unfolded and draped to dry on the grass under the Linden Tree. When seated, Elm and Stone asked Ciswen for a story. Albert rolled his eyes, coughed. Ciswen, lips curled, deepened her frown, and glared at Albert. The sisters laughed. They leaned back into the grass under the Linden Tree.

"We've been hearing rumours, troubles on the way. Trouble with a capital T," said Elm. She stretched her long legs and dug her toes into the earth. Overhead, the boughs of the Linden Tree rustled in the breeze.

"Never mind this soft, gentle place," said Stone. She glanced at her sister then said, "Outside Hidden Valley, an ill wind blows east."

Ciswen said nothing. She watched the sisters. She ignored Albert. "We stopped in to see Magda the Wise, and she reminded us," said Elm.

"To hear again the tale of the three tests," said Stone.

Albert sat up straighter and leaned in toward the women. The sisters Elm and Stone smiled their slow slant smiles.

"I've heard of these tests," said Albert. Ciswen closed her eyes.

Elm and Stone said, "All of Magda's tests bring either reward or harm, and the chance to barter. Seeds for stories, stories for seed!" Elm and Stone started to giggle.

Ciswen opened her eyes and said, "You two are experts in barter, in any case." Elm and Stone laughed.

Albert looked at the women: their laughter provoked him. *This afternoon is not going to plan! How dare Ciswen, oafish woman, ignore me. And these two sisters, mere washerwomen.* He noticed that when Elm laughed, her small sharp teeth showed pearly white. He noticed that when Stone laughed, a delicate rippling sound, she covered her red lips with one brown hand.

"Ciswen," the sisters said in unison. "How fine your leather apron! Smooth-grained and never scuffed with marks of wear and tear." Ciswen said nothing. She looked down at her huge hands.

"Ciswen, I know your leather apron is from Norway," said Albert. "Magda bred and killed and flayed. She cut and measured and cured the leather. She bade you to find someone whose heart was broken and then to mend the hurt." Ciswen looked first at Albert, then she looked up to the boughs of the Linden Tree.

Elm and Stone smiled. They looked at each other. Neither sister mentioned the hours Ciswen spent at her forge, hammering and filing a penknife in iron, gold lettering on its handle, *noli me tangere.* Neither mentioned Magda the Wise not being able to read.

In their mind's eye, sister to sister, having once trekked up the mountain pass behind Hidden Valley, they saw Magda in her hut, penknife gripped in strong brown hands, ripping open sealed parchment, inner scripts revealed and made decipherable.

Touch, rip, lift: words formed into shapes Magda could understand. And all the while she'd mutter, "Never fill your heart with too many words. You'll lose your wisdom." All this the sisters remembered. Instead of speaking, the two sisters stayed silent, until finally they said in unison, "Ciswen, in return for the leather apron, you forged a penknife for Magda the Wise!"

"So much talking under this tree," said Ciswen.

"We could tell our stories," said Elm and Stone in unison.

Ciswen stared at them and said, "How sly you two are! I know what story you are really after!"

All three women laughed together, long and loud. Not one looked at Albert the Mendicant, whose cheeks turned beet red.

"You and Bramah the Locksmith!" said the sisters.

"What of it?" said Ciswen. She sipped mead and munched on an apple. She wondered how to get rid of her guests.

"Magda made you promise you'd pick a lock to help Bramah with a stolen treasure chest!" said the sisters.

"Well, what of it?" said Ciswen.

Again, Albert's fingers longed to pull from his cloak pocket his tiny notebook. He wanted to know more about the treasure chest. He tried to arrange his face into a smooth smile that showed no resentment or concern. Albert's busy brain remembered how Bramah's drill and pick and file came not from Ciswen, but were a gift from the Pluto Seer on the night of the Wolf Moon at the time of the winter Solstice. Albert sat very still. He didn't want his thoughts known by the sisters Elm and Stone.

The breeze grew into a wind, and the boughs of the Linden Tree shook down a handful of glossy heart-shaped leaves. Attached to each leaf, the tiny buds of the linden flower, sweet and fragrant. Ciswen smiled and rubbed the buds and said,

"Bring us the bees, and bring us Bramah." Albert struggled to keep any eagerness from livening up his eyes. Elm and Stone knew to feign sleep. The more they pretended to sleep, the more sleep seemed to settle in under that tree.

And then Ciswen spoke.

"Once upon a time there lived a very old Linden Tree in the middle of a high meadow beneath a towering mountain topped with a huge ice cap. And one summer's night, after the first moon, Magda the Wise met me at this very spot, and I told her this story."

Ciswen's Tale about the Girl Who Never Lied

When I walked the Hidden Valley, my hammer encased in leather tapped against my hip. Tap. Tap. Metal to skin to cloth to flesh to bone. Each step brought me closer to our Linden Tree. Oh, I love the span of it, the girth of it! Here in the centre of the meadow. The afternoon sat still as a stopped clock. Everything vibrated with a rich silence.

Could the tree hear my approach? I'd not admitted to anyone, save to Bramah the Locksmith, how the Linden Tree seemed to grow and yearn toward my approach. Who would ever believe me, if I were to say that I heard words whispered on the wind, *Come, stand inside my green embrace.* I obeyed. I looked up into the dancing green boughs. I let my hammer slide to the ground. With three long slow breaths, I kneeled into the grass.

This ancient tree formed a sun-dappled cave. Chickadees chattered, and a robin somewhere high above sang two clear notes. I could taste the musky scent of late-summer honey as a thousand bees darted in and out, their pannier sacs filled to overflowing with pollen.

Someone coughed.

Eyes wide open, I jumped and reached for my hammer.

Under the boughs of the Linden Tree, a bench materialized and on the bench, a girl.

I peered in wonder. One minute, only me and the bees. And then, in a flash, there appeared a girl seated on a bench made from the tree's fine-grained wood. Carved in the bench were the shapes of puppets, shields, guitars, clarinets, and shuttered windows. Long ago, I'd heard stories about this bench and that if one was lucky enough to see it, there would appear a girl with it. Her name was Tilia. She wore a crown of tiny yellow linden flowers, and a felted tunic of linden bark beaten, dried, and stretched to fit her delicate shape. When visiting this tree, Tilia always brought a jar of honey as a gift. In a small silver flask, she carried two cups of lime-flower tea.

"Come, Ciswen," said Tilia. "Seat yourself down beside me. This ancient Linden Tree will soon change, and you will help it!"

My eyes widened, and although I was twice the size of the girl, I did as I was told. Then Tilia told me a tale — may Bramah forgive me for giving away secrets!

Tilia's Tale of Bramah the Orphan

Once, on a midsummer's night, far away and long ago, a young girl named Bramah ran toward the Linden Tree. With each step her cries echoed across the meadow. Grandmother had just died.

No one in this whole wide world loved Bramah as much as her Grandmother, and now, Grandmother was gone. With each sob, Bramah's tears watered the Linden Tree. Each teardrop fed the roots of the tree; each root pushed deeper into the soil, and then a strange thing happened.

The secret heart of the Linden Tree welcomed the lineage of Bramah's tears, for encoded within was the DNA of Bramah's Grandmother. And with it, wrapped tight in Bramah's tears, a hundred stories of the Banyan Tree that once grew in Grandmother's garden. The Banyan Tree was known far and wide as Aunty Bania.

Aunty Bania could talk. In Grandmother's days, talking trees grew everywhere. Each new trunk grown by Aunty Bania formed when her roots, which sprouted in the air, reached down to the ground. The more anyone cried under the Linden Tree—migrants on the run; Swords banished from Perimeter; beggars doomed to sweep Perimeter's mansions; children bereft of their parents—the more the roots of the Linden Tree welcomed Grandmother's previous graft: Banyan Tree DNA rubbed onto splints wrapped round with cotton scraps from Grandmother's saris and bandanas.

Albert, whose efforts at pretend-sleep, were, he thought, colossal, opened his eyes and coughed out, "Preposterous!"

"These things could happen then," said Ciswen. She leaned her back against the trunk of the Linden Tree.

The sisters Elm and Stone sat up, too. Elm said to Albert, "Oh, didn't we tell you about Aunty Bania?"

Elm and Stone's Tale about Aunty Bania

Long ago, after drought and famine, the monsoon arrived early. On the outskirts of a small town, on the far plains of Gujarat, in north-western India, Aunty Bania would laugh and say to Bramah's Grandmother, "When my green hair grows long enough to bind this town, that will be the time for you to leave." And so it came to pass that Grandmother left the town on a journey from India to towns and villages across Europe. And in her apron, she took with her roots from the hair of Aunty Bania.

Bramah's Grandmother, hired out as a migrant, worked hard in all her sojourns, from town to town, until she settled in Perimeter. Those were the days of on-call factory hires; gig economy offers. Grandmother took them all. She cleaned and cooked and seed-saved and stayed out of trouble. When the Wars started, the factory where Grandmother worked was bombed, and she joined, on foot, thousands who fled by train or boat. Grandmother's potions and skills with thread were well known. And one night, in a migrant camp, an army major commandeered her as a healer.

"You know," said the major, "I can get you out of here." He blew cigarette smoke into Grandmother's face.

Grandmother said nothing. She kept her head down, and her hands steady, binding the wounds of a young captain. Her name was Rahelia the Fiery, named for her red hair. Rahelia, wounded and nearly fainting from pain, sat up and said to Grandmother, "Don't listen to him." Then Rahelia passed out. The major shook his head, stamped out his cigarette, and stalked out of the Medi-Tent.

Of Rahelia the Fiery, many tales were told: her feats on the battlefield, legendary. Some say she fought for Consortium only on contract, just like Bramah. Some say, when Bramah comes to us again, Rahelia will be with her. Let the Resistance be strong!

Days later, feeble but back to battle, Rahelia visited Grandmother. "Your hands are warm," said Rahelia.

"They do what I tell them. At least for now," said Grandmother.

Rahelia wondered at Grandmother's age. Grandmother smiled. She paused in her work labelling and packaging dried herbs. She pushed back a strand of silver hair.

"Things will get worse here," said Rahelia.

"Yes," said Grandmother.

"When I send word for you to come, make sure you bring all that you wish to carry."

"I understand."

Nights later, on a huge transport plane, Grandmother sat and smoothed the folds of her skirt with many pockets. In each pocket, sewn into a square of patched cotton, small packets of seeds and the tiniest roots of the Banyan Tree.

"I'm always the first to say that immigration has its uses," said Albert. Ciswen glowered at him. Albert shrugged.

He took special care when saying this to keep his face smooth as a peach and his hands nowhere near his pencil. Later, alone in his small, rented room above the Hidden Valley Inn, on the outskirts of Perimeter, Albert would write everything down. He'd write so fast, smoke would curl up from his pencil!

Albert turned to Elm and Stone, and asked, "Wasn't there a rumour that Grandmother's seeds survive to this day, and in this very meadow, come the harvest moon, if you know the right spells, you'll find tucked away, just a few feet from here, beans and peas and squash?" Ciswen's gaze burned a hole into the clever hearts of the sisters Elm and Stone, and they stayed silent.

Albert, though, asked, "Well, never mind about the seeds, what about this crazy notion of tears feeding a tree's roots?"

"Oh, everyone knows that works!" cried Elm and Stone together. "You need to know the spells and when to say them, solstice to science and in between," the sisters said.

"You're telling me this Linden Tree is also an Aunty Bania Tree?" asked Albert.

"Of course," said Elm and Stone and Ciswen.

There followed a learned discussion between Ciswen and the sisters about the science of tree grafting and the preservation of hybrid roots, specifically related to the horticultural history of Linden and Banyan trees. Albert fidgeted, quite beside himself, and then, with a flourish and a great deal of coughing, whipped out his pencil and wrote with a fervour never seen by his pencil either before or since. Save that one time later when he wrote all this down.

Alas, all that remains of Albert the Mendicant's Tale are parchment fragments tacked up here on the wall of this mountain shack.

How cold this north wind blows! Dry as a desert, no moisture in the air. Green banished from our sight, we promise-keepers for seed savers journeying east to west—

There they were under the Linden Tree—

Albert The Mendicant Remembers Ciswen Telling Another Tale

Albert looked down at his notebook crammed with words. He closed his eyes, careful not to turn his head to the far meadow. Later, on his return journey, when Ciswen was back at work at her forge, he'd search each inch of grass to find those plants, to get at those seeds.

Ciswen smiled at Albert and continued Tilia's Tale:

Ah, the young Bramah. Alone in the world. She took safety under the Linden Tree, remembering how it gave shelter to her Grandmother. It was much younger then, but still the branches gave protection, the flowers' scent brought the bees, and the bees led Grandmother to the meadow. She ripped open her seams and from her apron came bean and tomato and squash seeds. These she planted and up they sprang. *Look again at this meadow,* said Tilia, seated on her bench. She looked straight at me. *You will find hidden in the tall grasses any number of bean and tomato and squash plants.* Tilia then told me another tale about Grandmother.

Ciswen Recounts Tilia's Tale of Grandmother

One night in mid-August, at the midnight hour, gangs of warriors tried to burn down the Linden Tree. The warriors had wanted to stop the Linden Tree from harbouring and giving safety to migrant workers and seed savers. Grandmother found strength among both workers and savers. In time, she rose as a leader.

"Aunty," the migrants and seed savers would call, "Crust, mantle, core!"

And Grandmother would reply, "To the bellows, my friends, to warmth and seeds to grow!"

She fought well and hard, but, in the end, Grandmother was one old woman against many battle-hardened warriors armed with picks and axes and swords.

The one weapon Grandmother had, though, was the knowledge of how to unlock the secret power of the Linden Tree. As the warriors bound Grandmother in chains, to be taken far away, she chanted 'The Secret Spell of the Cult of the Linden-Bania'. At the sound of Grandmother's voice, the many long branches of this very tree reached out and snatched Grandmother away from the grasp of the warriors.

The Linden Tree enveloped Grandmother's tiny, wizened body so that no matter how hard the warriors swung their axe, the Linden Tree repelled all cuts. Grandmother prayed and chanted one hundred different spells. Enraged, the warriors tried to bomb the tree. They shot sprays of chemicals at the trunk and boughs. Still the Linden Tree, although scorched and withering to brown, resisted. The warriors, like many violent men, were very lazy, and soon grew tired of fighting a tree that would not break or fall.

When a bugle call sounded yet another battle, these warriors ran off to burn and break all the settlements far past Perimeter. Grandmother sat down in the meadow, the better to catch her breath and rub her aching hands and feet.

Soon the King of the Far Meadowlands heard about the Linden Tree. He sent spies to watch Grandmother, but, before they arrived, the Linden Tree whispered, dream-like, that Grandmother must flee. When the king's men reached the Linden Tree, there was no sign of Grandmother.

Grandmother found her way to Perimeter. She met and married a good man, a farmer, and together they raised many vegetables and saved seeds. The farmer had a daughter, Miriam, from a previous marriage.

One day, when Grandmother's husband was on his way to market to sell vegetables and to barter for seeds, a band of robbers ambushed him. They beat him and stole his vegetables and all his seeds. They left him for dead, although he'd had the sense to roll away from their most vicious blows. The gash on his temple seeped red onto stone. As he lay dying, Grandmother's husband thought about his only child, Miriam.

"This proves another theory of mine," interjected Albert the Mendicant. Ciswen and the two sisters glowered at him. They said, "Never mind your theories." For once, Albert stood his ground. Quite literally. He stood up, cast his eyes across the meadow, and said, "Every good man will one day come to a bad end." With that, he turned his back on Ciswen, and the Linden Tree, and the sisters Elm and Stone. He'd had quite enough of Ciswen's tales for one afternoon. He wanted to get going. He wanted to get going to return by the light of a late full moon. He'd show that huge, ungainly blacksmith a thing or two about hunting for lost seeds hidden in some Linden Tree meadow! Although he'd not said another word, Ciswen smiled at Albert and shook one strong finger at him. Her laughter echoed after him as he made his way out of Hidden Valley.

If we were to rely on Albert the Mendicant for more information about the fate of Grandmother's husband, her stepdaughter Miriam, not to mention the remaining tales of Bramah, Tilia, and Ciswen — well, who would be foolish enough to do that?

See, here, tacked to the lower corner of this mountain shack, the tale of Miriam as recorded by an anonymous scribe decades ago:

The Scribe's Tale about Miriam

When Grandmother's husband didn't return, she set out in the dark of night and found his poor, beaten body. With his last breath, he said, "Find our seeds. Save them!" And then he died. Grandmother searched every town on the road to Perimeter, but she never did find the lost seeds.

Time passed. Grandmother worked the farm by herself. Some days, Miriam helped. But Miriam, an only child, was spoiled and lazy. Her hands remained soft as silk; her hair, black and shiny, cascaded over her shoulders. Her lips were red as cherries. Miriam loved to go to market.

Everyone within Perimeter, and in all the towns outside Perimeter, gossiped about Miriam, her wiles and her ways. Everyone looked askance when her belly began to show. No one ever knew the name of her lover. When Miriam's daughter was twelve weeks old, on the day of her Naming Ceremony, attended only by Grandmother and Miriam, a terrible East Wind started to blow. Grandmother shuddered. The East Wind were a harbinger of Aunty Pandy. Grandmother locked all the shutters.

She told Miriam to stay inside their small house. She brought out bars of soap. Miriam took one look at the soap and said, "I must go and get milk and honey for my daughter's Naming Ceremony." Grandmother pleaded with Miriam not to go, but Miriam said, "Mother, you can't stop me!"

So, Grandmother made Miriam a cloth mask and bade the young woman to wear it. She told her not to get close to the merchants nor anyone else. Miriam promised and set off, wearing her mask, to the town market. She bought her young daughter a jar of Linden honey and a pint of fresh creamy milk. When Miriam returned, she started coughing. One cough led to another, each deeper and rougher than the last. Grandmother put away the jar of Linden honey, folded up the clean linens.

"We will delay the Naming Ceremony," Grandmother said, her voice small and quiet. She forgot about the fresh creamy milk and left it to stand, sweet to sour, curdling. The shadows of evening grew darker. And Miriam coughed and coughed. Grandmother made Miriam a poultice of ginger and honey. She made Miriam lie down. She rubbed and stroked and never left her stepdaughter's bedside. All the early hours of that cruel day, Grandmother tended to her only next of kin, a stepdaughter not her own, yet ...

At the sound of the third rooster crow, Miriam's breath rasped and rattled deep in her chest. Then, she died. Grandmother, her face lined with furrows, cried one solitary tear. It was the last tear she ever shed. *Now,* Grandmother thought, *now there can be no Naming Ceremony for my daughter's daughter.*

In the next room, the Girl with No Name cried and cried. Grandmother stood in her humble home and listened to her crying granddaughter. Grandmother looked at her dead daughter lying under thin cotton sheets. The baby's cries filled the air. Grandmother washed her hands with soap. She put on gloves. She kept her mask on.

She stripped her daughter's body and washed it clean. Then she burned all the bedclothes. When the townspeople saw Grandmother's bonfire, they arrived with a cart and took Miriam away. Grandmother stood and watched the cart drive off.

Outside, that East Wind blew, and Aunty Pandy laughed her cold, coughing laugh.

Inside, Grandmother washed down her small wooden house made with oak and neem, and seamed with the pitch of boiled banyan roots. With her soap made of lye and wood ash, Grandmother washed the floors from noon to night. She ripped cotton and sewed her own masks.

In the coming days, she took care of her granddaughter, the Girl with No Name. Grandmother only went out once a day to get food. Almost everything else Grandmother made at home or bartered. A whole year passed, and then one bright summer's day the town crier announced, *Aunty Pandy's good and gone!* And everyone came out into the streets, save Grandmother.

Grandmother went on doing what she had always done: she planted seeds and grew plants and sold the plants. She made soap and saved the glass jars that she bartered for with the plants and the seeds. She bartered for cotton and sewed masks. She kept away from everyone, except her granddaughter — *the Girl with No Name.*

Ciswen sighed and turned to Elm and Stone. "When next you wash the clothes of the townspeople of Perimeter, down there by the river, be sure and tell them this tale!"

And the two sisters nodded, their faces sombre. Silence filled the valley. The leaves of the Linden Tree trembled. An East Wind began to blow —

— **icy and unforgiving!** If only snow would fall again, rich, thick, wet. Before you set out again, see here this fragment pinned to the wall of our shack; warm yourself with these words:

One day, when the Girl with No Name was twelve, Grandmother took the girl to be apprenticed to the Locksmith, Joseph P Bramah. But that is another story for another day.

Today, all you need to know is that on August 14, once a year, in honour of Bramah's Grandmother, Bramah and Ciswen meet beneath the Linden Tree that is one part Banyan, said to be a thousand years old. Everyone from far and wide in Hidden Valley, including even a few reformed warriors tired of killing and destruction, will gather with the tradespeople and seed savers and a handful of the settler-farmers in the Valley. Everyone will assemble for Linden Honey Mead served from the huge barrels of aged oak. Everyone will eat huge slices of Sachertorte, cut and served by Ciswen herself. Everyone will savour cupfuls of basmati rice with saffron and ghee, from Grandmother's secret recipe hidden away deep in a crevice in the lower trunk of the Linden Tree. Many stories will be shared, each one tucked inside the other, just like this one.

Detention Centre C
Inside Perimeter

Logbook, drone disabled:
as noted by the duty guard
"We found no trace of them,
save for one tattered page,
frayed, ripped in half —inked writing almost invisible —"

FEATURE INTERVIEW

Renée Sarojini Saklikar

Pulp Literature: *'Told under the Linden Tree' is a companion story to your epic fantasy in verse* Bramah and the Beggar Boy. *Could you tell us a little about how this poetry/prose side story came to be?*

Renée Sarojini Saklikar: This companion tale actually preceded volume one of my epic fantasy in verse, *Bramah and the Beggar Boy*. I have been working on a children's story featuring mythical characters that I've re-imagined from the tales told to me as a child. The premise for these tales pivots around that question, 'What would happen if . . . ?' What would happen if I let my childhood memories of stories from different cultural traditions merge with research into climate change and ecology? That's how 'Told under the Linden Tree' first got started. So there I was, working away, when I got the call from Jen at *Pulp Lit*: would I consider a 'side tale' from the Bramah epic? Happiness! That magic of doing the work, just doing it, trusting the process. You never know what will happen, what opportunities will come your way.

PL: *This story addresses catastrophe and loss — of the environment, of human health, of language and knowledge and culture. Do you believe that we have already fallen over the precipice of no return, or is there reason to hope?*

RSS: Such a powerful question, terrifying and important. My incomplete understanding of our cultural moment, of the science and the warnings, is that it may well be too late for us humans. And also, "Hope is the thing with feathers" (Emily Dickinson). As a preacher once said to me, "Hope doesn't secure the present, it enlarges the future."

As long as there are makers among us with the capacity for compassion (from the Latin, *to suffer with*), maybe we'll have a chance?

While writing this, I googled a fragment lodged in my memory, from TS Eliot's *The Wasteland*. Toward the end of the poem, Eliot offers us hope through three words that he draws from the fable of thunder in a Hindu source. To escape the wasteland, Eliot says, we must *datta* (give), *dayadhvam* (sympathize), and *damyata* (surrender control).

PL: *In 2018, you published* Listening to the Bees, *co-authored with scientist Mark L Winston. In some ways, 'Told Under the Linden Tree' feels like a gentle reminder that we should also be 'listening to the trees'. What can we, as citizens and stewards of this planet, learn from our arboreal companions?*

RSS: To have patience, to listen even more deeply. Trees have the longest lifespans and the longest circles of memory!

PL: *We were delighted to publish your short story 'Man with Golden Helmet' in Issue 28, Winter 2021. And we are thrilled to share more of your work with our readers. How have the events of the last two years impacted your stories and poems and the way you choose to tell them?*

RSS: Deep thanks to *Pulp Literature*. I loved merging a ghost story with memoir, and the brilliant editing team at the magazine guided and helped that vision into print. The pandemic impacted me in oh so many ways, large and small, tragedy and great gifts. I'm still processing. And am doing so with profound gratitude for all who have laboured so hard to keep us safe.

PL: *Your projects range from large-scale creative works, such as* thecanada?project *and the Thot J Bap series, to pens-on-the-ground activities such as the Lunch Poems poetry series and the Surrey International Writers' Conference. What keeps you hungry for poetry? What nourishes you and allows you to continue to serve the writing community?*

RSS: The hunger is as air is to breath. To serve is to be healed. Took me a long time to get that. Some days are better than others, though.

PL: *On a lighter note, what are your favourite words and aphorisms?*

RSS: Hah. I can never really answer questions like that! It changes with the season and the hour.

PL: *If you could choose one book (other than your own) for every child or teen to read, what would it be? What about for every adult?*

RSS: I'm far too superstitious! Perish me to choose. Let all who find story find what brings joy.

PL: *What words of wisdom do you have for new writers just getting their literary feet wet?*

RSS: A preface before I answer: some years ago, I read a *New York Times* article, the gist of which was that to live a beautiful life, never give advice. And yet sometimes a random word at the right time catches us and keeps us going. So here goes: believe in your work and listen to the work. In the end it's not about us — it's about the work.

PL: *Thank you so much for making the time to speak with us. Before we go, do tell: what are you working on now?*

RSS: You are so welcome. An honour to be asked! I'm working on book three of the Bramah series, having sent to my publisher book two, *Bramah's Quest,* forthcoming in spring 2023.

§

Selected publications of Renée's can be found at thecanada?project: thecanadaproject.wordpress.com/books-and-collaborations

Information about Renée's epic fantasy in verse is available at thotjbap.com

For a recent biography, visit the Poetry in Canada website at poetrycanada.org/board-biographies

NOTHING LEFT ETHAN'S PECS

Finnian Burnett

Finnian Burnett *teaches undergrad creative writing and English. They've published several novels, but their true love is flash fiction. Finnian has placed in or won contests with Bath Flash, Bridport Prize, Blank Spaces Magazine, and Reflex Press. The Clothes Make the Man, a flash fiction collection about Arthur, a trans man navigating academia, was recently released by Ad Hoc Publishing. Finnian's next collection is forthcoming through Off Topic Publishing. In their spare time, Finnian watches a lot of Star Trek and takes their cat for walks in a stroller. Finn lives in BC with their wife and Lord Gordo, the cat.*

Nothing Left

The squad comes while Random is away. Random feels it, perfectly aimed shots piercing Callie's neck, severing her head from her body.

The men shoot until Callie lies in pieces. Random watches through Callie's neural processors. They click and whirr as she lies dying on the floor of the little home they built on the outskirts of the largest human city.

"That was the last one in the eastern sector," Random hears a man say through Callie's ears.

"Good," says another, laughing.

They gather Callie's parts and leave, scuffing the cheap vinyl flooring Random lovingly laid. For a moment, she marches with them through the last of Callie's awareness. Then nothing.

Random steels herself and marches down the mountain, not bothering to hide from the squads, not consulting her internal database to access troop movement. Let the bastards come. Let them kill her. She has nothing left anyway.

When she reaches their home, Random finds nothing left of Callie but half of one hand. The men didn't even bother to tear down the leaning shack they've lived in the past few years.

Always in fear, always in love. The men were wrong. Callie wasn't the last. Last year, a passing sentient told them of an entire community of biomechanics living in massive settlements in sector Z.

Random curses herself for not looking for the others earlier — she'd been too caught up in loving Callie to take the risk of going on a hunt for others like them. Random cradles the partial hand in her arms, rubbing it against her cheek. Maybe she does have something left to live for. Revenge. She kisses the metal fingers and whispers goodbye.

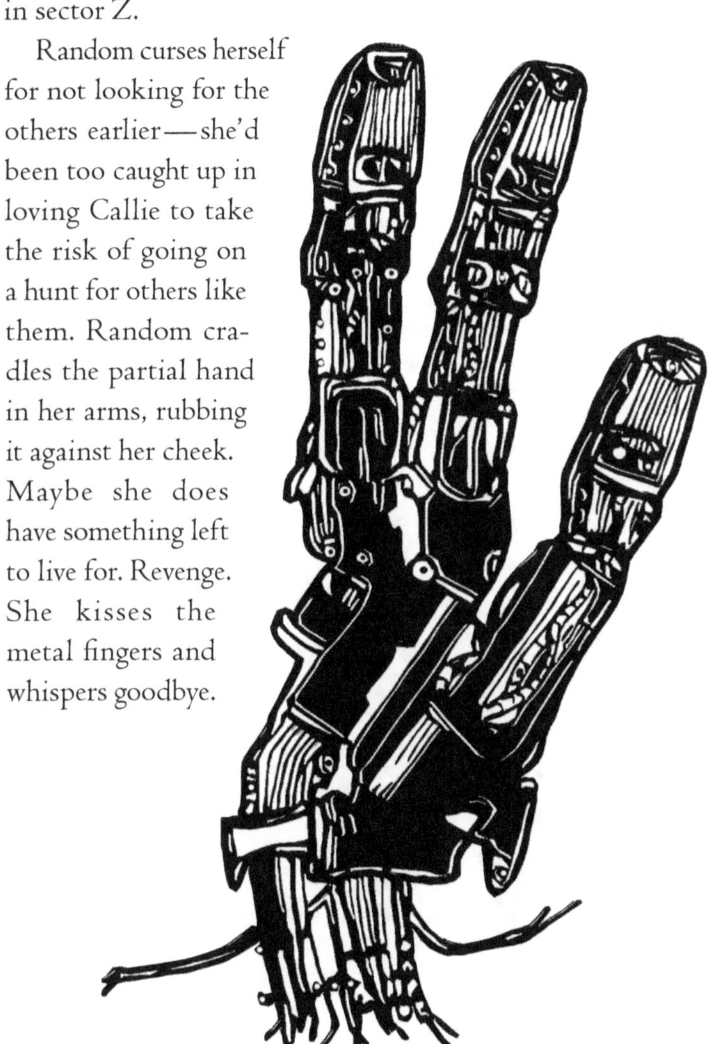

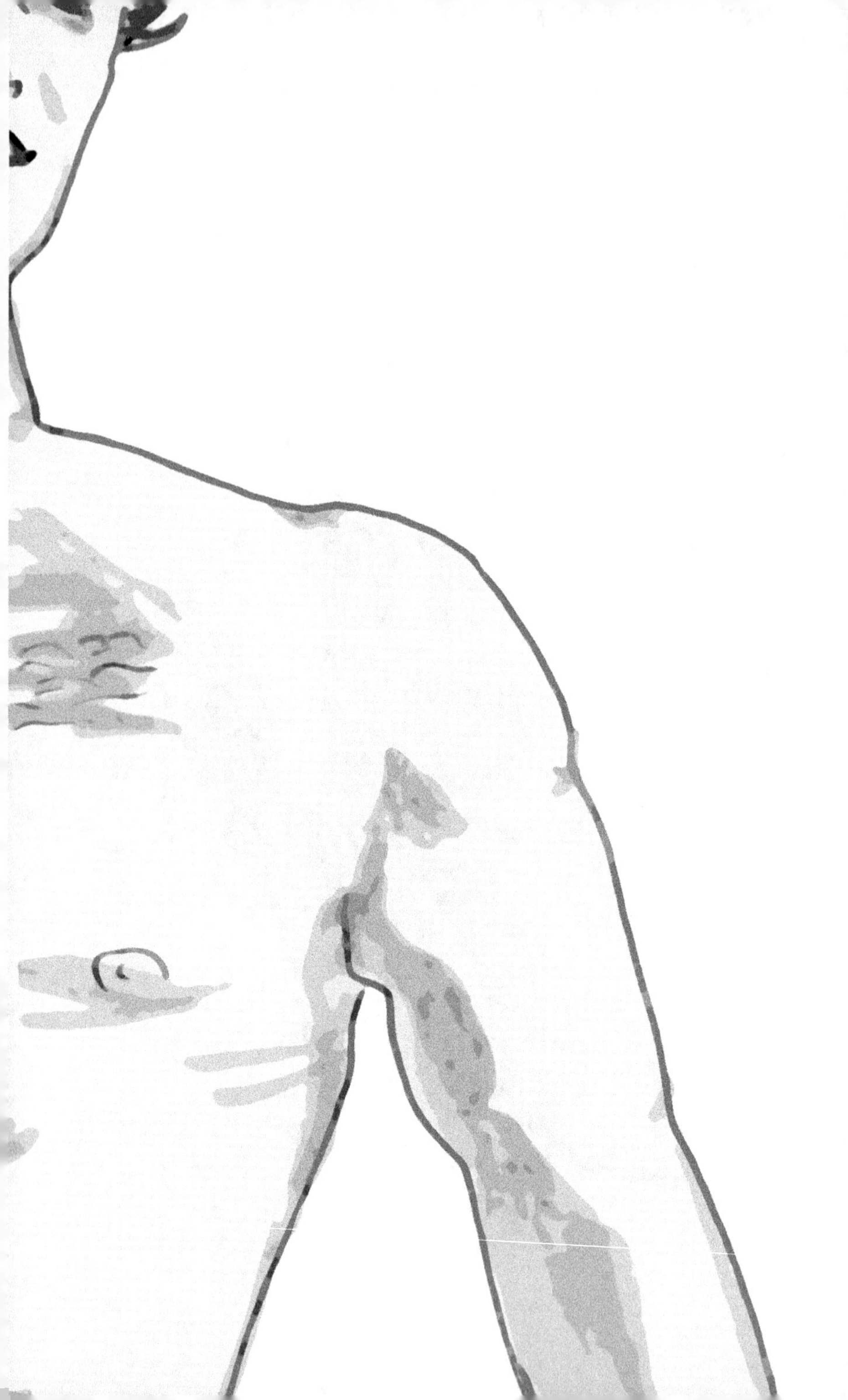

Ethan's Pecs

Ethan Peck flexes his muscles on screen, and Candice sighs next to me because he's so dreamy, so tall, so gorgeous. It's not the actor she loves, it's Spock, the character he plays. That's what I tell myself when Candice says, "Isn't he perfect?" And he is, he's perfect, so perfectly male, and Candice's palms rub circles on the thighs of her jeans as Ethan speaks his deep-voiced logic, tightly controlled emotion simmering under the surface, and Candice leans toward the TV, eyes wide, and Ethan's such a man, such a deep-voiced man, and I slide deeper into my oversized button-front shirt, trying to hide the side-boob flab that has escaped my binder.

She falls in love with him over and over when he comes on the screen, and *I'm right here*, I want to say, but instead, I watch the show and listen to Candice's sighs and when it's over, she rubs her fingers over my sparse new beard and says, "I love you, Devin," and she does. I know she truly does.

ZARA'S SONG

JM Landels

JM Landels *is the author of the bestselling Allaigna's Song trilogy, the final book of which,* Allaigna's Song: Chorale, *has just been released from Pulp Literature Press. 'Zara's Song' is the mirror story to 'Gwannyn's Song', which appeared in Pulp Literature Issue 35. You can find @jmlandels on most social media platforms, or at jmlandels.stiffbunnies.com.*

Zara's Song

The breeze off the water is balmy here in Rheran compared to the northeasterlies that scour Caella at this time of year. But Zara pulls the black cloak tight across her chest anyway, shivering from a chill that has nothing to do with wind. The clank and rumble of the anchor chain seem to vibrate through her tightly wound body. She watches the cog sway off into deeper water, carrying the sleeping Princess High of Brandishear, Gwannyn.

Former Princess, Zara thinks, correcting herself. *Or former Gwannyn.* That role, and that name, are Zara's now.

There is a strange ache she feels in the centre of her being, knowing she will never see or speak to her double again. It is the part she has trained most of her life to play, in a play that has been in production longer than she's been alive. As a child, she dreamed of being an actor — of fame and adulation, and of being admired for her talents. She will have fame and adulation, but none must know of the talent she brings to this role. She feels destiny settle on her shoulders and seep through her body, wrapping her more tightly than the cloak.

As the cog makes its way out of the seagate, she lifts her head higher, blinking away the windborne salt spray.

The cloak helps her walk unnoticed through the streets of Rheran to the Bastion. She has studied the city in maps and drawings, and through the murky lens of a scrying crystal, but nothing prepares her for the riot of colour and noise in this southern port city. Unlike the straight, broad streets of Caella, the alleys here twist and turn, shopkeepers' wares tumble out onto the pavements, and hand carters stop wherever they choose to sell their goods. Even this early in the year, the streets away from the water are warm enough to make her want to doff her cloak, but she doesn't dare. It is not just the plain black fabric, but the charms woven in with the threads, that make people's notice slide off her like rain from a new-oiled sail.

On impulse, she takes the longer route, exploring her new city before she reaches her home. In truth, she knows she is delaying the first test of her disguise: passing herself off as Chanist's wife and mother of his children.

She walks past a confectioner's and the name tugs her memory: Herron's. Gwannyn has mentioned it in her reports. Perhaps it is best to test her disguise with lower stakes. Unaided by charms, she lowers the hood of her cloak and steps through the doorway.

"Your Highness." The shopkeeper smiles and curtsies.

"Good afternoon, mistress," Zara says in Gwannyn's voice. She can't remember if the shopkeeper has a name other than Herron, but she calculates that Gwannyn, born into royalty, wouldn't bother with the names of shopkeepers. Still, at her first opportunity, she must begin reviewing all her extensive notes.

"I've some of your favourites, freshly done," the shopkeep offers. She pulls a tray of brightly coloured candies — red, purple, orange, and blue — from the shelves behind her. "Try one. I infused this batch with lime."

Zara hesitates, her hand hovering over the tray. She is surprised to see the candies are in fact flowers. She picks up a purple one she recognizes as a violet, and nibbles it. She tries not to make a face at the strange floral taste buried beneath too much sugar, and smiles instead.

"It's lovely," she lies, despite the sinking realization that however much her face and voice match the first Gwannyn's, their tastes are different. Yet another aspect of herself she will need to retrain.

For a moment she lets herself feel the hollow weight of despair at the enormous scope of her task and the enormity of the treason it entails. She nearly lets slip a tear for Gwannyn, asleep on the cog.

The very least Zara can do is be the best counterfeit mother she can be.

She stretches her false smile wider. "I'm not here for myself, though."

"And what will please the young princesses and prince today?" asks the shopkeeper.

"I promised them lemon drops," Gwannyn replies.

Zara shuts the door to her garderobe and locks it from the inside. She closes her exhausted eyes and slides her back down the door, allowing herself to sit for the first time all day. The carpet beneath her is thick and soft, and she buries her fingers in the dense wool. She doesn't need to open her eyes to know it is the finest carpet she has ever been allowed to tread upon.

She recalls the lumpy rag rug in the attic room her mother rented when she and her brothers were children. That was before the damp dirt floor of the shack near the river and the cold, unfurnished stone she slept on when she was apprenticed to the Mageguard. The threadbare carpet of her room in Rose Alley was the most luxurious thing her feet claimed till now. But here in Rheran, the wool that Elalantar raises cushions the pampered toes of princesses, while its people tread bare boards and shiver through icy winters.

She allows the old, familiar rage to rise up and push away fatigue. She opens her eyes, and the blood red of the carpet matches her anger. She tugs off her shoes and stockings and stands, defiantly barefoot, in the deep pile, unable to stop herself from luxuriating in the relief it gives her tired feet. She gazes around the opulent dressing room of the woman she is here to impersonate. This, then, is her reward. Not for the task she still must do, but for everything she has suffered till now. She knows the hardest part is still ahead of her, but the reward for that will come years from now, when her people are free from the tyranny of princes. Till then, she will enjoy every boon the affluence of privilege affords her.

Arrayed in one of Gwannyn's—no, *her*—loveliest gowns, she inspects herself in the mirror. She is as like the first Gwannyn as two women can be, and the charm she cast on herself has brushed away any remaining differences in appearance. The perfume she dabbed on her throat and forearms is her husband's favourite—according to Gwannyn, who she can only trust hasn't lied to her—with a few added drops of one of Zara's own tinctures, proven to make her near irresistible. She must be careful to linger only with her husband when she wears it. Unless there are some more delectable courtiers. She chases the thought away. There will be time enough for other men and women. First she must secure Chanist's heart as her own.

She is all but ready to meet her husband of seven years for the first time. But there is one more duty that comes first. She passes her hand in front of the mirror, and the silver ring on her little finger glows. The mirror goes dark, seeming to suck the light of the room with it.

Ondrade appears almost instantly. He's been waiting, and she can see the furrowed lines of worry and impatience on his brow as clearly as he recognizes her in the mirror.

"Gwannyn," he says. "How goes the day?"

"It is I, Zara," she replies, and then remembers to give the code word. "Roses."

His shoulders sag in relief. "You're late. Has there been a problem?"

Zara shakes her head. "Not as such. She is safely aboard the *Bessie*. I watched it raise sail."

"So why the delay?"

"I needed to familiarize myself with these chambers — and to rest — before my toilette." She omits the other delay, when she encountered her children for the first time. It was lucky she had the lemon drops, for they provided a distraction when she needed to cast her first set of charms, earlier than expected and unprepared as she was. The young ones had been easy, but Lauresa, the eldest, had a stubbornness of mind and a piercing gaze that unnerved Zara. For the first several weeks, she will need to charm all the children every time she sees them. After that she will be able to decrease the frequency. Lauresa, however, might take longer.

She closes the part of her heart that rails against the need to enchant the minds of children. *It is a kindness, in the end,* she reminds herself. *They'll never know the loss of a mother.*

"Gwannyn — Zara — are you all right?"

She pulls her face together, dabbing at the corners of each eye to be sure her maquillage remains untouched by tears. She nods at Ondrade and puts on a smile. "I am better by the minute." She waves a hand in front of the mirror, dismissing him.

She adjusts her hair and her smile, unlocks the garderobe door, and prepares to meet her husband.

§

The years have been kind to Gwannyn's face, but not to her soul. She wonders from time to time how the other Gwannyn fares. She no longer thinks of her as the real Gwannyn, but simply as an earlier version, like matching dishes made by the same potter: different to look at, perhaps, if side by side, but essentially the same.

The Gwannyn-who-was-Zara has retained the beauty she brought with her to Rheran—has improved upon it even, by dint of creams, lotions, and charms—but it is a quiet beauty. When she first arrived she used magic to make herself less noticeable, avoiding the attention of others lest she reveal cracks in her disguise. Now, she no longer needs magic to disguise herself, and the quiet self-effacement has become a habit she is too timid to shed. It has been five years since she stole the first Gwannyn's life, and any differences between the two of them can be attributed to time. If the other Gwannyn turned up at the lintel of the royal apartments now, who would be seen as the impostor?

Soft and quiet is simply her mode now.

She aches when she watches her stepdaughter Lauresa, grown to a stunning young woman, sparkle and glow with the court's attention on her. *That could have been me*, Gwannyn thinks, forgetting, as she does often these days, that she was not born a princess.

But Ondrade is quick to remind her of the poverty from which the Mageguard rescued her, and of the lifelong plan that will in turn rescue their people from the same. And then she reminds herself to be grateful for the luxurious life she leads, for however long it lasts.

In the autumn of her sixth year in Rheran, Gwannyn's sister comes to visit.

Princess Cyrnan is High Admiral of the Elalantar fleet now, and the visit is as much a strategic and state affair as a family reunion.

Cyrnan's embrace is warm and familial, though utterly unfamiliar. "It is good to see you, little sister," she whispers into Gwannyn's ear.

Gwannyn says nothing but returns the embrace with as much warmth as she can muster through the fear that seizes her belly.

Later that night in the royal apartments, Chanist leaves his wife and sister-in-law to their reunion. Gwannyn has made the obligatory inquiries after their parents and cousins, blessing her excellent memory. It is jarring to hear the woman she knew as her Queen spoken of in filial exasperation and affection. And even stranger to glean personal details of Elalantar's consort, who was a cipher to her when she lived in Caella.

Cyrnan refills their glasses from the half-empty decanter of Myrwater red. "You know," she says, "I thought you'd died."

Fear seizes Gwannyn's belly again, and she takes a sip—a tiny sip, for she needs her wits about her—wondering what turn she needs to take next to maintain her deception. "Whatever would give you that idea?"

Cyrnan puts down her goblet and leans forward, elbows on knees. Gwannyn is struck by how much Cyrnan resembles

Gwannyn's younger daughter, Miani. "Around five years ago, give or take," Miani says in a voice so low Gwannyn is forced to lean forward herself, "do you remember me writing to you, asking you to recall the name of the weaver you used to see in Rose Alley?"

The cold knot of fear twists tighter. It had been in her first month at Rheran. The arrival of a letter from Gwannyn's sister had forced her to plunge into a collection of old correspondence to create a convincing reply. The query about Gwannyn's erstwhile lover — the one she should be at that point reunited with — was worrying. Zara crafted a reply to Cyrnan, giving Nazzedh's name and asking fondly after him. There was nothing else she could write that would not arouse suspicion, and she waited several months for a reply. But the next letter from Cyrnan made no mention of Naz at all.

She makes light of it. "It did seem odd, sister, since you yourself introduced me to Naz. You never did carry my regards to him, did you?"

Cyrnan shakes her head. "I'm sorry, Gwannyn — I had no time. There was … a lot … going on at the time. And after, I simply forgot. I wrote that letter to be sure you were alive. Once I had your letter, and our spies confirmed your safety, I had a puzzle to sort out."

Gwannyn leans back in her chair, arms crossed. "Spies?"

"Don't give me that look, sister. You have yours at Caella too."

Gwannyn tips her head. That is fair. And Cyrnan doesn't know the extent of it. "What puzzle?"

"In the late winter of that year, a private vessel was shipwrecked off Farwiel — the *Bessie*. The crew abandoned ship, and no crew member has been found who survived that day.

But there was one person left behind, strapped to a bunk and consigned to the sea." Cyrnan gazes down at her hands as if searching for words.

Gwannyn's guts have tightened to the point they have strangled her voice. There is grief there, for the Gwannyn who never made it back to Naz, but overwhelming that is the desperate scramble for what her words must be when she has to speak.

Cyrnan looks up. "It was you."

Gwannyn forces her eyebrows up and gives a small laugh. "Clearly not!"

Cyrnan shakes her head. "Her face was swollen with seawater, and bruised and cut from the force of the waves and wreckage, but I know my own sister. Or at least I thought I did."

"Are you saying I have a twin out there?"

"That's exactly what I'm saying. It was pure chance that my ship was the nearest to the wreck. Farwiel is nearly as close to Rheran as it is to Caella. I was this close to sailing straight here and confronting your husband. But Mother and Father deserved to know. So I wrote that hasty letter to you, to see if my eyes somehow deceived me, and sent an inquiry to our ambassador in Rheran, inquiring after your health. And I sailed home to Caella with what I took to be my sister's corpse."

Gwannyn knows she should do something sisterly here to offer comfort for the grief Cyrnan has so clearly felt, but she is paralyzed by the clashing implications and just beginning to grieve for her children's mother. "How awful," is all she can murmur.

Cyrnan continues. "I sailed into Caella and had the corpse taken to the mortuary. Under cover of night, I moved it myself to our family crypt. Before I brought Mother and Father there the next day, I inquired whether they had had news from Rheran.

Nothing. No word from you, nor from the Bastion at all that anything was amiss. When Father saw the body, he collapsed on the floor of the crypt in his grief. But Mother's reaction was different. She brought both hands to her face and stood staring at the corpse while tears leaked between her fingers. 'This is not Gwannyn,' she said at last. And she told Father and me a story she'd shared with no one before.

"You did have a twin, Gwannyn. But she was stillborn."

Gwannyn's heart stops ever so briefly, and when it restarts the world has changed, and she with it. She sets her goblet down with utmost care, her hand shaking despite her effort. She stares at the two cups on the table, hers and Cyrnan's, two nearly identical vessels by the same maker.

"How?" she asks, not raising her eyes, not even sure of the question she is asking.

Cyrnan's reply sounds distant, as if she's speaking across an ocean of time.

"I remember when Mother was pregnant with you. She was sick and weak like I've never seen her before or since. Her belly was huge for her time, though as a child that meant little to me."

Gwannyn interrupts, suddenly impatient. "So she was obviously pregnant with twins. Why was I never told?"

"I don't know. Why wasn't I? I don't even know if Father knew. It was only when I told her about the corpse with your face that I learned any of this from Mother." Cyrnan picks up her goblet, drains it, and puts it back beside Gwannyn's. "When Mother went into labour with you it was far too early. The midwife used her magic to save your life. But she could only save one."

Gwannyn looks up at last, not bothering to hide the angry tears filling her eyes. "Then how do you explain that adult corpse?" She knows already, but she wants to hear her sister say it.

"I spent several months investigating, but it seems the midwife who attended your birth stopped catching babies afterwards. I gave up. But a few weeks ago, I attended the arraignment of a notorious pirate. This was among his possessions." Cyrnan reaches into her pocket and draws out a ring. She places it on the table. "It was Mother's. You wouldn't remember it, because she gave it to the midwife who saved your life."

But Zara does know the ring. Her own mother wore it on a pendant around her neck. She had wondered more than once why her mother didn't sell an object of such clear worth to lift their family out of poverty. She waits for Cyrnan to continue, not trusting herself to speak.

"A pirate's word may be trusted only so far, but the one object he requested to keep was this ring. He said it belonged to his mother, who died this spring."

Zara's tears are unstoppable now, for the lowborn mother she lost, the royal mother she never knew, and the sister whose death is on her hands. As for the sister in front of her, who comes around the table to put her arms around her … she wants to unburden herself to Cyrnan, to tell her that she, Zara, is that twin, but how can she? The web of lies she has constructed is too complex and too fragile to risk pulling a single strand. Instead, she allows herself to cry on her sister's shoulder until she is empty.

She cannot go back. Reality is what she has written. Zara died on the boat, and she is now the only Gwannyn. She has everything she always wanted. She is a princess in truth, with none left who can gainsay it. So why does it feel as if her world has ended?

When at last they break apart, Gwannyn bends to pick up the ring. "The pirate," she asks, already knowing the answer. "What is his name? And has he been hanged?"

Cyrnan shakes her head. "I would not risk his life till this puzzle is fully unravelled. He is Xaddien Ken, of the Seawitch."

"I would ask you grant him clemency," Gwannyn says. "For it seems he is a relative of ours, if only by adoption." She puts the ring on her finger where it glints gold next to the silver one. "May I keep this as a reminder of the sister we never knew?"

"Of course," Cyrnan says, and hugs her sister again.

§

Like a rat that keeps finding new crevices through which to enter a home, Lauresa's daughter is back. Gwannyn managed to cut short the child's pagehood here at the Bastion when the girl stabbed her cousin in a street brawl. But then Allaigna turned up again less than three years later, somehow finagling her way into one of the Ranger corps. Gwannyn tolerated that for six years — the Rangers, after all, spent hardly any time within the walls of Rheran — but when Allaigna mustered out, Gwannyn convinced Chanist to send Allaigna on a one-way mission to the wilds of Oburakor, along with the other threat to her children's inheritance, her husband's grand-nephew. Gwannyn patted herself on the back for the tidy way she sent two potent risks away in the company of her Ilvani agent. Whether the mission succeeded or failed, her agent would keep both potential heirs well out of the way until her own daughter Perran — she thinks of them all as her own now — can ascend as Princess High of Brandishear and Gwannyn can complete her work.

But Allaigna is back, with no word of why or how from the Ilvani agent.

Gwannyn closes the garderobe door behind her and seats herself at the vanity. She waves a hand in front of the mirror, and the ring on her little finger glints with its familiar pearly light. There is a longer wait than usual, and Gwannyn drums her fingers, fretting out her worry.

At last her reflection dissolves and is replaced with Ondrade.

"Your Highness," he says with his twist of a smile. "The hour is late. To what do I owe the honour?"

Gwannyn frowns. "If I had time for games, I wouldn't be contacting you at this hour." She adds, "Sir."

"Well then, report."

"My contact at the Errelyte Order informs me Genissa has had a visit."

His eyebrows shoot up. "From whom?"

"A woman. Tall, dark hair, pale skin."

"You think it is she?"

"Who else is likely?"

"Then we'll have to move faster than planned. Is Kolluk'khan ready?"

"She's made excuses and retired early from dinner. She says it can be done by tomorrow. As soon as we've heard the petitions, Chanist and I will set sail to visit my family, and I'll return a widow."

"Well enough. I suggest you go back and enjoy your last meal as consort."

Gwannyn tips her head and sighs, ever the consummate actress, hiding her impending grief. "It was nice while it lasted."

"It lasted more than two decades. I hope you're not too used to it."

She shakes her head. "My loyalty to the Guard is unchanged."

He smiles his grim twist again. "As is ours."

She wants to stay here, to allow herself to weep for the husband she must betray and the life she must leave. But she doesn't dare. If she starts to cry now, she may not stop, and time is of the essence. Tomorrow, when petition day is over, she will use all her wifely charms — and if those fail, her magic and the mage Kholluk'khan's — to convince Chanist to set sail to visit her mother, the Kingfisher Queen, Princess High of Elalantar, on her deathbed.

The only balm to her conscience is that she has changed the plan. She will not assassinate her husband, for Kholluk'khan will aid her in casting magics stronger than ever before. Stronger than those that fooled an entire royal household into thinking Zara was Gwannyn; stronger than those that clouded Lauresa's mind and made her forget her mother and her young suitor, Chriani; and stronger than those that have influenced Chanist's hand and policies over the last two decades. This time, he will forget himself entirely and live a humble life on the Isle of Canthya. But at least he will live.

Gwannyn wakes with a mix of unease and sorrow swirling through her body, a feeling that only grows with the hours. It is petition day, and she and Chanist will have to sit and hear pleas, complaints, and demands, while all she wants to do is walk through her home and say goodbye. She will return, but not as Princess High, and not with Chanist.

She takes her chair beside his on the dais and reaches over to squeeze his hand, blinking away the disobedient tears that want to swim upward. He gives her a brief, distracted smile. There is something different about him today, but she can't quite put her finger on it. It is no matter. In a few hours time they will be on board the ship to Canthya.

Gwannyn scans the room for the high mage Kholluk'khan. Her dark face and golden vizier's robes should be easy to pick out from the crowd, but the mage is not here. Gwannyn breathes, settling her nerves. She trusts her friend and vizier is already at the docks, preparing their way.

When the first petitioner's chit is drawn, Gwannyn is unnerved once more. Lauresa's daughter Allaigna steps forward, bearing a long cloth-wrapped bundle across her arms. The young woman is not supposed to be here, but Gwannyn is prepared. She has rehearsed the ways she will deflect any contact between Chanist and his granddaughter.

"Grandfather," says Allaigna, dipping her head. "Your Highnesses." She looks at Gwannyn and manages a bow despite the awkward bundle she carries.

Chanist clears his throat. "Allaigna, my darling. What petition might you have?"

"Two things, your Highness," the young woman replies. "I bring you a gift on behalf of your brother's wife."

Taerysh. Gwannyn wonders what the old she-wolf is up to and chides herself for having lost track.

Allaigna proffers the bundle. The wrappings fall open as she lays it at Chanist's feet, revealing a sword, which Gwannyn has no doubt belongs to Taerysh's grandson Goffree. "She demands justice for her grandson's death."

Gwannyn feels her world tipping and sliding through the hammock of schemes she has woven. Goffree and Allaigna should still be in the wilds of Oburakor, alive or dead but out of Chanist's sight and mind. The reappearance of his grand-daughter with his grand-nephew's ashes has reawakened a part of him that Gwannyn thought long since laid to rest.

"I would you'd told me this in private, Allaigna." Chanist takes a breath that restores his composure. "What is the second?"

The woman in front of them steps back and raises her voice for the benefit of the room. "I have composed a new lay. Parts of it have been sung in taverns and halls from here to Teillai. But it has not been performed in its entirety. It would be my honour to sing it here for you, Grandpapa."

Gwannyn's nerves scream with danger. If Allaigna has merely a glint of her grandmother's talent, her spellsinging could unravel the decades of charms threaded through the minds of the entire court, and especially Chanist's.

She should have had Allaigna and Goff killed outright. Or she should have ordered Allaigna assassinated when the girl arrived back in Rheran. But Gwannyn has a mother's heart now, and Lauresa, however estranged, was her daughter for a time. She puts her hand on Chanist's wrist, squeezing it as if she can compel his will through touch. *Do not listen*, she begs silently. *We can be happy still.*

Gwannyn's grand lifelong plan to overthrow the principalities of Brandishear and Elalantar lies in ruins. But it was never hers. She was chosen before birth for this role. She wonders if Ondrade and the other puppet masters of the Mageguard will allow her to live, and whether the safest place for her is here, imprisoned in the Bastion.

Allaigna found the way to her grandfather's heart, and he allowed her to sing a lay, right there on petition day. It bared all the machinations of the Mageguard, of the court and High

Council, and of Gwannyn herself. Gwannyn was imprisoned, and her husband was shot.

They have not treated her ill. She is in a small room in the south tower — away from the hidden corridors of the north that could lead her back to her apartments. Kholluk'khan has fared worse, she assumes, for the Colleges are not kind to viziers who break their oaths. Gwannyn wonders if the mage will be hanged. She thinks not. There is a weariness to Chanist's heir, Allaigna, that says she has seen too much death lately. But Irdaign, Chanist's first wife, is now the power behind the throne, and Gwannyn cannot read her.

Chanist. Chanist is not dead, though nearly all who were in the room that day must think it. The stonebow bullet that struck him was wrapped in more layers of enchantment than Gwannyn could parse in the ensuing chaos. And she has no doubt Irdaign's ministrations of the corpse were lifesaving and life-disguising magic. It soothes Gwannyn's wrung-out heart to know he lives, though it is an additional wound to know she will never be allowed to see him again.

How foolish she was to permit herself to love him. And her children. When did she stop being their caretaker and become their mother? Her deception has been revealed. Do they hate her for it? She wants to tell them that even though she didn't bear them, she would sacrifice everything for them. Not because she is their aunt — a truth that none but she will ever know — but because her heart has become Gwannyn's.

She begins to laugh, softly at first, then louder, and then unstoppably. Her plans lie in ruins, she is stripped of her crown and her ambitions, but her family is safe, and she couldn't be happier.

For more magic and intrigue set in the lands of the Ilmar, check out the spellbinding conclusion to the Allaigna's Song trilogy, Allaigna's Song: Chorale, on sale from Pulp Literature Press: pulpliterature.com/product/allaignas-song-chorale/

BLAZE OF THE UNIVERSE

Jude Neale

Jude Neale *is a master educator, Canadian poet, vocalist, spoken word performer, workshop facilitator, and mentor. Jude has written eleven books to date. Her latest book is called* The Flaw. *Her book* A Quiet Coming of Light: A Poetic Memoir (Leaf) *was a finalist for the Pat Lowther Memorial Award, a recognition of Canadian women poets. Jude's piece 'About Light' appeared in* Pulp Literature *Issue 13, and we are delighted to share another of her poems. This one was shortlisted for our 2022 Magpie Award for Poetry*

$\mathcal{B}$LAZE OF THE UNIVERSE

Did Mozart know
he was writing music
that would put
my babies to sleep?

Did he see the light
glaze pass over
their faces as they heard
the soft tinkle of bells,

hidden in twinkle twinkle
little star? Me humming,
soft as down, this refrain
over and over. They suckled,

bluest of blue eyes,
closing with each breath.
I chanted the ending:
how I wonder what you are.

I could feel the peace swelling in the room,
violins and piano:
and you, Amadeus, jubilant,
playing complex patterns

And ellipses, knowing
this was the last dance.
You played for royalty,
and for all the sleepless

children to come. They lay
stilled in their mother's arms.
They didn't cry, but dreamed
of the holy blaze of the universe.

REGARDING LINE 25600 OF YOUR INCOME TAX RETURN

Cadence Mandybura

Cadence Mandybura's *fiction has been published in* Orca, FreeFall, NōD, Fudoki Magazine, *and the* Bacopa Literary Review. *Cadence is a graduate of the Writer's Studio at Simon Fraser University, the editor of the Federation of BC Writers'* WordWorks *magazine, and the associate producer of* The Truth *podcast. Three of her award-winning stories appear in* Pulp Literature *issues 29 and 35. Learn more at cadencemandybura.com.*

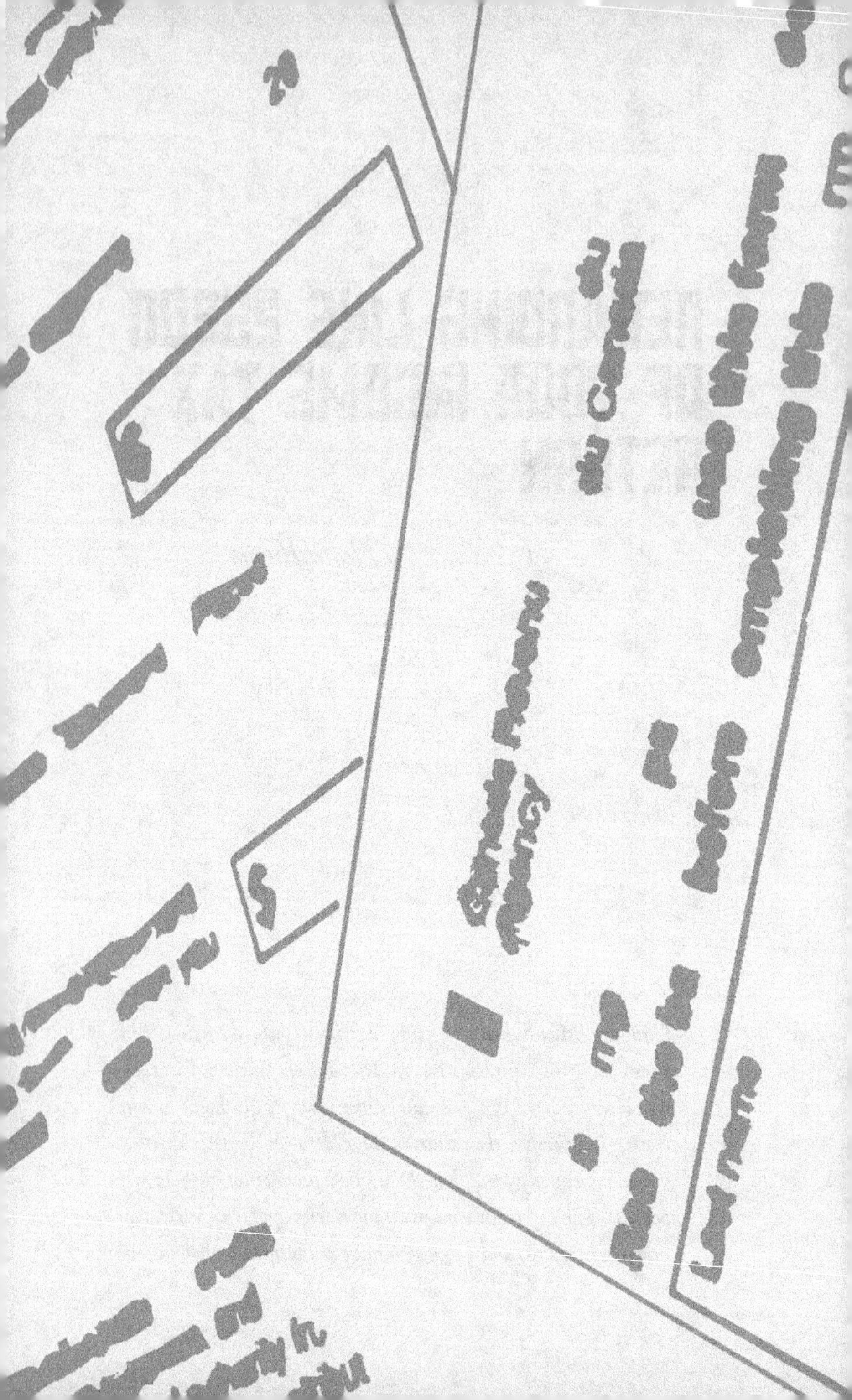

$\mathcal{R}$EGARDING LINE 25600 OF YOUR INCOME TAX RETURN

The auditors arrive on your doorstep first thing the next morning, the speediest government service you've ever received. They ring the bell three times before you drag yourself from your cereal to the door.

There are two of them, a man and a woman, dressed in neat grey suits with fresh-pressed morning smiles. The man has a clipboard, the woman a rolling kit parked behind her.

"I'm Auditor Kapoor, and this is Auditor Lavoie, from Revenue Canada," says the woman. "Are you Mr ——?" She rattles off your full legal name, your social insurance number, and the income you reported in box 150 of your tax return less than twelve hours ago. You confirm the information warily. "Excellent!" she continues. "We're here about your vows."

"What?" you say. It's 8:30 a.m. on a Sunday: the time of self-pitying hangovers, not government reviews.

"Your taxes, sir," clarifies the man, Auditor Lavoie.

"Yeah?" You pinch the bridge of your nose. "I just filed them last night. I made the deadline, I'm pretty sure."

Specifically, you filed with nine minutes to spare, Ottawa time. Even though, by then, the bourbon was dissolving your grasp on space and time, you had checked the clock. It was the last time your taxes would show that you and Alessia were still married. Still lived at the same address. Still mixed your money together as easily as your imagined futures. No trace of that Rahim guy anywhere.

"We know," says Lavoie pleasantly. "You did."

"Your tax refund was filed correctly, for both yourself and Ms Liberi," says Kapoor. "We're just here to enforce your tax vows."

"Perpetual poverty is first on the list," says Lavoie, reading off his clipboard.

"What are you talking about?" Memory rouses like a cranky cat. "Oh, that was ..." A joke? "... a mistake."

Sort of. You were nettled by DynamoTax's increasingly esoteric interrogation of your life and finances. When it asked if you had taken a vow of perpetual poverty, you had checked YES with bitter humour. So much of your income leaked away over the years, into renting space and filling it with stuff you and Alessia had acquired. She had left most of it behind, and you were sick of your furnishings, down to every last teaspoon. Perpetual poverty didn't seem like such a bad idea.

Admittedly, checking the perpetual poverty box was probably the smallest of your mistakes last night. You shouldn't have left your taxes to the deadline, with no runway to sober up. You *really* shouldn't have used them as an excuse to call Alessia. What was it you asked her for, anyway? Her receipts? They were in the file she had prepared for you a month ago, she told you calmly. Which you knew. Which she knew you knew.

Perhaps you thought there was some healing magic in the

tax code. After all, Revenue Canada was willing to consider you and Alessia common-law partners long before you were emotionally ready for such a label. Next year, you and Alessia can look forward to ripping your finances apart again. If only bank accounts could bleed and scar over to mark the occasion.

"Look, just fix it. I'll pay whatever I owe."

"Hmm … no … According to our records, there was no mistake. Everything was perfectly correct," Lavoie says, glancing at Kapoor for validation. She nods, then lifts a hand and signals behind her.

Cleanly choreographed, the two auditors pivot to the side to let two, four, six … shit, well over a dozen movers barge into your home.

"What the hell?" You try to step in their way, but they brush past you with ease. You're not up for a physical altercation, with every movement a cymbal crash in your hungover brain. While the movers seem friendly, they are clearly much, much stronger than you. They begin cheerfully packing your belongings.

"Where are they taking my stuff?"

"Why don't we step outside?" says Auditor Kapoor. "We'll go through the details with you."

"Be careful with that!" you shout at a mover who has picked up a stained-glass lamp, one of Alessia's thrift-store treasures. He grins and gives you a thumbs up. When you turn back to the doorway, the auditors have stepped into the scrubby side yard of your duplex. They smile expectantly. Cursing under your breath, you shove on your runners, struggle into your windbreaker, and wince at the sunlight as you step outside. Out here, the gulf between the auditors' clean professionalism and your unshaven shabbiness seems wider than ever.

"You can't possibly do all this," you say. "Over a clerical error!" Your tongue isn't awake enough to navigate the tricky sounds of 'clerical', but the auditors pretend not to notice.

"We'll give you instructions on the grievance process later," says Kapoor.

"But we have a lot more to get through first," says Lavoie, brandishing his clipboard.

"Seriously? Hey — *hey!* That belonged to my aunt!" you shout as the movers cart away your TV stand.

"Please, sir, let's focus on completing the vows. Then we can address your grievances," says Kapoor. Then, perhaps taking pity on your confusion, she adds, "Everything goes to a secure government facility. It'll be safe until you've worked through the necessary paperwork."

She nods at Lavoie, and he presses onward. "Vow of poverty underway," he says, marking a restrained check on his clipboard. "Next, let's see … It says here that you vowed that you were done with women, for real this time, and that you would never *ever* fall in love again."

"Excuse me?" Your questions rev forward all at once and come out in a pile-up. "You couldn't've heard that. Do you have my home bugged or something? I never said — I mean — there's no fucking *box* for that on the tax form!"

"It is unusual, yes," says Lavoie, his cheeks pinking at your aggression. "But we get a few cases like yours every year." Immediately, you regret swearing at him. He looks young, less sure of the job than Kapoor, who has turned to pull something out of her kit.

"Look, I just used a program — everything was preset. I couldn't have added anything like that," you say in a calmer voice, your tone wobbly.

"That may be, sir, but it came through quite clearly on your tax forms," says Lavoie.

Kapoor pulls out a contraption that looks a bit like a Soviet-era Super Soaker—a goofy rifle with a big tank, painted concrete grey. "Now, this shouldn't hurt," she says, and points it at your chest. Before you can even flinch, she flicks a switch. The device emits a flatulent beep, and you feel a small pop somewhere in your chest.

As she clicks a small canister off the gun, your hand drifts to your sternum. You feel about ten grams lighter.

"What did *that* do?"

"Extracted your capacity for romantic love, per your vows," said Kapoor, pressing a label to the canister with her thumb. "It's not as bad as it sounds. My neighbour had hers removed a few years back, and she's never been happier." Both the gun and canister disappear into her kit. "Next?"

"'*I'll get a dog. Dogs are loyal. Dogs love you. No matter what,*'" Lavoie reads from his clipboard.

"Right," says Kapoor, reaching back into her kit and lifting out a squirmy puppy. "Here you go."

You accept the warm little body because you can't exactly refuse when someone hands you a puppy. It licks your chin. Some of the movers notice the dog and smile.

"And you'll need this too," Kapoor says, handing you a canvas bag heavy with dog food and supplies. Your hands are full of puppy, so she places the bag at your feet. "I'm told it's a boy," she continues. "No name on record, but we were talking about it on the way over. We think Peanut would be cute." She grins, then snaps her professionalism back into place. "Just a few more items to resolve, I think."

"'*Tracey, Tracey, where the hell are you? I'd call you up right now, no joke,*'" recites Lavoie faithfully.

"Dialling," says Kapoor, holding a phone to her ear.

"Wait, wait, wait," you say. Hearing your eleventh-hour words spoken back to you in sunlight makes your stomach churn. "I haven't talked to her for fifteen years — I can't just —" Yes, you did think of Tracey last night. First you wasted several hours scrolling through Alessia's Instagram, trawling for any pictures of Rahim with dates that overlapped with your so-called marriage. Finding none, you started looking up other women from your past, anyone with whom you'd had even the most tenuous sexual potential. From what you could dig up, a lot of them were married already, or clearly out of your league. But you couldn't find Tracey in the swarm of her namesakes, and you never kept track of her after university.

"Hi, is this Tracey?" Before you can stop Kapoor, she mentions your name and your mortifying (private! drunk!) desire to reconnect. Ignoring your frantic, one-handed *no-no-no* waves, she hands you the phone with a bright, "Here she is!"

And you take it, bumbling the puppy over to one side because it'd be rude to leave Tracey hanging like that.

"Hello?" you say.

"*Hi!*" she says, prompting you to pull the phone a few inches from your ear. "I can't believe you're still thinking of me after all these years! I had no idea you were still in town. I'd *love* to meet up!"

"Uh …"

"In fact, I'm having a little party Saturday afternoon! Do you need any vitamin supplements? I've gotta tell you about this amazing new smoothie mix, and I'll be doing a demo. No pressure, of course, but everyone who's tried it positively *raves* about it …"

You let her rattle on about the smoothie mix and special pricing, your perforated heart tickling with memory. Right. There was a reason you never asked her out. "Uh, Tracey?" you mumble, balancing the phone and the puppy as you watch the movers cart away your mattress, then your bed frame, then the trunk you always bruised your shins on. "I can't make it. I've, uh, taken a vow of poverty. Gottagobye."

You hand the phone back to Kapoor, then return your attention to the creature in your arms. Peanut is cute as hell, but you're suspicious that his vibrating excitement means that he's about to pee.

"That was probably a good choice," observes Kapoor. "There goes your blender."

You spot the movers loading a box with saucepan handles sticking out of it. "Seriously? Oh, forget it. Let's get this over with."

"Certainly," says Lavoie. He licks his finger and flips to the next page. And then the next.

"Is there a problem?" you say, like that's a question that makes sense when your possessions have been apprehended, a piece of your heart has been sucked out, and you're now wholly responsible for a dribbly canine life. "Good boy," you mutter to Peanut. It's hard to stay mad when you're holding a puppy. Alessia liked dogs, you remember, but she was allergic.

"At this point, a lot of the vows become . . . inarticulate," says Lavoie, furrowing his brow.

"Not uncommon," says Kapoor sympathetically. She reaches out and scratches Peanut's head as you wait for Lavoie. You really need an Alka-Seltzer. Then you realize your bottle might be on the government truck already.

"Here we go." Lavoie clears his throat. "*You know, I guess what I want at the end of the day is for Alessia to be happy. That was really what*

I vowed to do at our wedding, right? I did want her to be happy. Do. Even if it's not me anymore … Maybe this Rahim guy … ugh. But I'd be an asshole to fuck that up for her, right? Yeah. Yeah. Gotta do what's right. Stop dwelling. Stay out of her hair. God, the hair she left everywhere. And the shower drain …"' Lavoie pauses and resumes his normal speaking voice. "It grows increasingly irrelevant from there."

Peanut is falling asleep in the crook of your neck, although you can still feel his tail wiggling.

One of the movers taps Kapoor on the shoulder. "We're done here, ma'am."

"Good work," she says. "We're almost through." She looks back at you. "Unfortunately, we don't have the resources to enforce that last vow. Austerity measures and all that." She rolls her eyes, and Lavoie grins. "But it's been officially noted on your file. Now, you wanted to know about the grievance process." She goes back into her kit and pulls out a three-inch binder. "The first step …"

"You know what," you say. Your mistake last night, you're realizing, wasn't about professing vows you didn't mean. It was believing that you can actually make things better. Just because you spent several $130-an-hour counselling sessions scraping gunk from your soul doesn't mean Alessia will love you again. More specifically, it won't make her stop loving Rahim.

"Whatever. It's fine."

The auditors exchange a glance. "You're sure?" says Kapoor.

You nuzzle Peanut. Remember Alessia.

"Yeah," you say. "Except maybe that bit with the gun?"

"Sure. We keep all extractions in a safety deposit box. You can collect yours if you come in with the right paperwork. Offices open at 9:00 a.m. Monday." She pulls a hefty pinch of papers from the back of the binder and tucks them into the bag of puppy gear. Then she holds up her finger, as though she's a cartoon character with an idea, and tosses her pen in the bag, too.

"You might need that," she says. "Our movers are very thorough." She checks her watch. "Anything else, sir?"

You rub your forehead. "I guess not," you say, adding an automatic, "thanks."

"Thank *you*, sir, for being so reasonable. Please call or email the CRA if you have any questions."

You wonder if you still have a computer or a phone, but you don't say anything, letting the auditors leave in peace.

Juggling Peanut to one shoulder, you pick up the bag of Puppy Chow and government paperwork and head back inside. Your place is empty, and your footsteps echo strangely. You put Peanut down, go to the kitchen for some water, and discover they've left you one of everything: one glass, one saucepan, one spatula, one plate, one fork, knife, and spoon. And two clean bowls.

You fill one with water and the other with kibble, then let Peanut eat up.

"Hungry little bud," you say as he digs in with chop-smacking eagerness. You sit on the floor and watch him enjoy his meal.

Since, indeed, you don't have a phone or a computer, you spend the day with Peanut, exploring your neighbourhood at a puppy's pace. The auditors provided a leash, treats, and plenty of dog-doo bags.

Everything from last year has been squared away, if rather more completely than you might have wanted. You're not sure what the vow of poverty has done to your bank account, but, you decide, that's a tomorrow problem. For now, you have everything you need.

SLIP INTO MY FUR

Patrick Barb

Patrick Barb, an author of weird, dark, and horrifying tales, is currently living (and trying not to freeze to death) in Saint Paul, Minnesota. He is the author of the novellas Gargantuana's Ghost, Turn, *and* The Nut House, *as well as the novelette* Helicopter Parenting in the Age of Drone Warfare *and the forthcoming dark fiction collection* Pre-Approved for Haunting. *Visit him at patrickbarb.com.*

Slip into My Fur

Your shoulder aches. Wooden splinters from the cracked door-frame decorate your close-cropped hair. The cabin's quiet during the off season. I imagine your ears ringing—your conflicted fight-or-flight working overtime. But don't worry, that's why I'm here. You fly to me so we can fight—together.

My place on the floor before the fireplace offers a terrible angle from which to see your features, but the hitching of your shoulders between the gulping breaths suggests tears falling. You're splattered with brown-and-tan mud, mixed with something darker, from your Doc Martens to your mid-section, helping me fill in the gaps.

Heavy rains the last few nights, a washed-out road. Easy enough to get stuck. Did you fall when you undid your seat belt and opened the driver's side door?

The rain and mud drips from your body and onto the floor. Did you walk? Or run? I hear your heartbeat through your soaked denim jacket, so you must've run.

You ran *to me*.

Takes me back to those years before, when the killer you called *Daddy* bellowed a primal scream with the force to shake branches and send nested birds flying. All because he found you with his taxidermist's daughter.

Back by the smoker, your hands, eyes, teeth, and tongue explored. Curious.

The cabin was open and the wind blew the right way. I heard your whispers, tasted the beads of spit caught between your tongue and hers, smelled your joy — and then, your fear.

Inside the cabin, you ran to me. Already strong enough to bear the weight, you lifted my fur, created an opening between my tail and back paws. Even though you should've been impossible to miss, a bulge under the bearskin rug your father thought of as his own, he never found you. I hid you until he passed out in his chair by the fire, spilling peaty-smelling liquor from an uncapped flask.

You crawled out and didn't look back, whispering, "Daddy?"

By the reflected image in my dead black eyes, I watched you put your head in his lap and tell him *you* were sorry.

I nuzzled and nipped my cubs. I nursed, but disciplined with a weighty paw when it was needed to keep them safe. When we wandered from the cave their first spring (our *last* spring), I was prepared to let them go. To give them a chance to make the world their own.

Your daddy flung those dreams aside in a volley of hot lead and foul smoke. My cubs lay bloody on the ground beneath. Their gore in my eyes and on my shattered teeth.

Pain next. Then black.

Until your face — round, soft, and held between your palms — appeared. You lay down on the floor beside me, in your basketball shorts and an oversized concert T-shirt, asking, "Was this rug a mama bear?"

Your daddy grunted, indicating you should play with dolls and leave him alone.

Bloody mud, a velvet soup like offal, sloughs from your shivering bulk and lands on my dust-covered hide.

Now you see me. Now you remember what I promised before.

I'm the bearskin you loved when you were a girl. I'm the bearskin who called your daddy a killer. I'm the bearskin who promised to be there when you understood.

Remember?

You fall to your knees. Hard to say if it's from exhaustion or because you want a closer look. Either way, we're face to face again.

Your eyes drift to the fireplace.

It won't work. Firewood's soaked by the downpour. It'll never catch.

"What do you suggest?"

I can't smile. Can't move. But imagine that's what I'm doing now.

So, you *can* hear me after all.

"I heard you crying … for your cubs. Late at night when he … when Daddy had to bring me here after Mama … after she …"

Silly girl. I wanted to stop *your* tears. Thought I had too many for us both.

"I'm done crying now," you say.

Yes, you are.

Tell me what happened. Strip off those ruined clothes and slip into my fur. I'll warm you.

Your voice isn't too different from the way it was before, only scratchier from screaming and crying. Still, I'm struck by this sense of the familiar as you narrate the next chapter of a story I haven't heard in years. But I haven't forgotten it either.

He said it was a phase. A sin. Said you'd get over it, move on. Sneering, he called you his linebacker beauty queen.

He refused to understand.

You cut him off, got as far away as you could, thinking that was enough.

Now, years later, he found you. A drunk, senile old man letting his foot *slip* on the gas. His old truck hopped the curb at top speed, ground your children and the woman you loved to so much blood and bones. You don't leave out a detail of your waking nightmare.

Your very own *natural* disaster.

You ran, seeking somewhere safe. Somewhere to hide.

Not as a means of escape, but as a disguise. A second skin, so the two of us can have our revenge.

Carry me on your shoulders. Drape me over your head. It's okay. Each step from the cabin and on the path is easier than the last. Even when my hollowed-out head covers your face, you find a way forward, seeing through my dead black eyes.

Together we're strong enough to lift your truck from the mire, throw it in reverse, and leave these woods for good.

The truck speeds down back roads until we reach streetlamp-lit neighbourhoods. A familiar home comes into view. We lose your thumbs in the final transformation. Thin, scabby fingers expand into my heavy paws. My fur tightens around you. The steering wheel jerks when we hit the mailbox.

We bump the truck door open and fall to the lawn on four legs.

It's been too long since I moved on my own. *Almost on my own.* You've got me, don't you?

We have each other.

Someone peers into the dark from an open garage. A scared old man fresh from the police station. Somehow you knew, *we knew,* they'd let him go and he'd be here.

"Not for long," we say.

The words come as a growl.

FALLING FOR YOU

Tom Jolly

Tom Jolly *is a retired astronautical/electrical engineer. His short stories have appeared in Analog SF, Daily Science Fiction, and MYTHIC and can be heard from wandering storytellers if you buy them an ale on a warm afternoon. You can follow him on Twitter @tomjolly19 and find more on his Amazon author page or his website, sites.google.com/view/tomjolly/home.*

$\mathcal{F}$ALLING FOR YOU

There were nine of us, all on our hands and knees or bellies, cautiously peering over the unprotected edge of the building's roof and watching Ralph fail to fly. He even tried to flap his arms, for all the good it did.

Man, I'd just learned his name five minutes ago.

"Well," I said unnecessarily, while belly-crawling back away from the edge, "*he* can't fly."

Which meant that of the nine remaining people, one of us could. At least, that's what the (evidently) evil Doctor Dead had written on the sign he'd left behind on top of the building. But he might have been lying.

It was difficult to guess how high we were; the tall structure had no windows, and we hadn't arrived here by stairs or elevator. We had been teleported here. We had all read the notice posted flat in the middle of the tower when we arrived: "Of the ten of you, one can fly. When you find out who that is, the rest will be saved. Signed, Doctor Dead."

We all exchanged glances, waiting for someone to announce that they could, in fact, fly. Janine, captured the same time I was, surveyed everyone with a critical eye. Gladys fretted with the edge of her knit sweater; Lucent stood with his arms wrapped around himself, looking lost, despite the bravado of his dyed red hair and piercings. Joshua sat with his face in his hands. And a hulking guy I mentally dubbed Brutus didn't seem bothered at all, just angry and calculating. Of the other two, a young man sat with his arms around his knees, sobbing, while a slightly older woman watched him from a few feet away. Ralph had seemed manically excited, like he was expecting a miracle.

Nobody announced that they could fly.

We speculated about the madman who wrote the message. Doctor Dead must have been one of those weirdos who liked to put people into situations where they were forced to kill themselves. It was a distinct subclass of psychopath. When the Big Change came through and gave so many people special powers, he apparently acquired the ability to teleport. It was a nice power if you were evil, since you could teleport anyone anywhere on a whim — in this case us, to the top of this strange building, surrounded by rocky desert dotted with patches of short brown grass. There were no signs of civilization that I could see, not even a dirt road or power lines reaching up over the horizon. The monolithic structure we stood upon was smooth and dark and featureless except for the sign. There was no safety rail. And our phones didn't work up here.

I wondered who put the tower here to begin with. It didn't seem like the sort of thing a psychopathic killer would do. Some of the Changed fancied themselves artists, so the tower might have been part of some artistic vision.

I didn't know how Doctor Dead was watching us, but it was a certainty that he was.

"So, if one of us can fly, why doesn't that person just jump into the air and try to fly?" Gladys asked.

I shook my head. "It doesn't always work that way. There are what are called stress-triggered abilities. They don't manifest unless the person is in imminent danger, say from falling off a building. One of us might be able to fly and be completely unaware of it until we're put in a situation where we might die. Just jumping straight up into the air won't help."

Perhaps that's why, as we debated theories and options, Ralph decided jumping off a building would be a good way to jump-start it. It was a mystery as to why he thought he was the one, but when the Change came through, a lot of people were depressed to discover that they weren't one of the anointed who were granted a special power, or convinced that they were deserving of it and that a huge cosmic mistake had somehow been made. Ralph must have thought to correct that mistake.

After the horrific spectacle of Ralph, we returned to the centre of the monolith and sat in a circle, gathered around the notice describing our special doom. Brutus said, "You know, I'm not going to starve to death up here. One way or the other, we need to find out who can fly so I can go home."

It was clear to all of us as his eyes scanned the group that, if necessary, he would toss us off the building one at a time until such a discovery was made. He was bigger than any of us. He could do it. Gladys said, "Do you realize that if you are the last one here, you will have to decide to jump off yourself?"

"Nine-tenths chance I won't," he said.

"Eight-ninths," I corrected. He glared at me. "It's a statistics thing. Sorry," I said, meaning to pacify him. "You only count the unknowns. Ralph is a certainty."

"Besides," Gary said with a tight smile, "you might not be the last one. You have to sleep sometime." Gary, with his thin blond hair and bland, puffy face, did not look like someone who might try to kill you in your sleep. But he did look a lot smarter than the words that had just fallen out of his mouth.

Brutus, threatened in this manner, stood up, grabbed a wide-eyed Gary by his collar, and walked to the edge of the building while Gary wriggled desperately. Most of the rest of us screamed uselessly at him to stop. Brutus tossed him over the edge. I felt a momentary insane urge to get up and take a run at Brutus, standing so close to the edge himself, but fear twisted my gut and I just stood there, paralyzed with everyone else while Gary screamed all the way down. Nobody asked if he flew.

Brutus turned and looked straight at me, and I cringed. "Seven-eighths?" he asked.

I swallowed and nodded, and refrained from mentioning that if one of us could, in fact, fly, then Brutus would go to jail for murder, as the flyer would escape to tell the tale. Of course, on our current track, we might all die, and maybe he was thinking about that instead of the consequences of his immediate actions. He didn't seem particularly bothered by it; it was as though he'd committed worse violence in the past.

We sat in a circle again, giving Brutus plenty of room. "There's got to be a solution to this," Gladys said, her voice cracking. She looked light enough to blow away, and I wondered if that could be counted as flying. She was at least sixty and seemed like the archetype of grandmothers. I had trouble imagining Brutus tossing her off the building without apologizing to her first. She kept glancing over at him nervously.

The young knee-hugger suggested, "If we all jump off at once, and one of us can fly, then Doctor Dead will save the rest of us before we hit the ground."

"Or," I suggested, "they're a lying psychopath, none of us can fly, and Doctor Dead will be jerking off somewhere, laughing maniacally and watching us as we all hit the pavement below." That produced a few nervous titters but mostly sour looks. "Maybe we can sit together and figure something out without killing one another," I added.

"Figure what out?" Brutus asked, sneering at me. "We're at the top of a . . . whatever this is, waiting to die. We got a couple of hours of daylight, and then it's nighttime in the desert. We'll probably freeze to death."

I looked around. It was noticeably cooler than when we'd arrived, and there was a light breeze. A couple of the people who'd arrived here in shorts and T-shirts already had their arms wrapped around themselves and their knees drawn up. Brutus was right. But there still might be a solution to the problem.

"Let's start with the basics," I suggested. "Does anyone here actually have any special abilities?"

"I can sing," one of the others said. "Kind of."

"I mean superpowers. Stuff we might be able to use to get out of here."

"Who put you in charge, anyway?" Brutus asked.

I sighed. "Nobody. But this is what I do for a living. I work at an agency that takes quirky special powers and finds a place for them. Markets them. If one of us has a quirk, maybe I can find a way to apply it."

"Better Hero, Inc," Janine said. "I've heard of you guys."

Janine was one of the first names I'd learned because we were teleported here as a pair. We'd been standing too close together in the grocery store, an easy double target, having a lively discussion on the best toppings for Triscuits. At the time, I was trying to work up the nerve to ask her, a complete stranger, out for coffee. I guess you could consider this abduction our first date, but I didn't really want to.

As the eight of us talked, several other conclusions came to mind that I wasn't quite ready to share with everyone else. We had all appeared here—the forced teleportation leaving us briefly unconscious—after some stranger wearing a balaclava and a white overcoat touched our shoulders. As with flight and strength, teleportation was fairly common among the supes. It was also one of the more valuable traits you could get. A lot of teleporters who wanted to avoid dangerous occupations got jobs in the transportation industry, carrying stuff from country to country. It paid well. So it was curious that someone with this ability would decide to go the 'evil' route. Or maybe it was just a sideline. Transport cargo during the day, murder people during your time off.

People rarely acquired two abilities. Only about one in ten people got any special ability at all, and most of those were crap. The likelihood of getting *two* special abilities was one in a hundred, three abilities one in a thousand, and so on. If our evil mastermind could teleport others, then it was unlikely that Doctor Dead could do anything else—like know what abilities we might manifest under stress. And without remote vision or super-vision or ghostly presence or any of that, they couldn't watch us kill each other unless they were physically present. That made it likely that Doctor Dead was one of the people standing here with the rest of us, acting all innocent, knowing perfectly well that if someone pushed them off the top of the monolith, they could just teleport safely away.

Additionally, if Doctor Dead only possessed one power, they probably had no way of knowing whether one of us could fly at all. It was just BS to make us murder each other or ourselves. An obscene game.

I couldn't mention any of this out loud and retain a chance of living through it. Once Doctor Dead was labelled, they would just flit away before we could throttle them. And if we killed them, well, how would we get off the building? Fly?

I chewed on my lip a moment as I looked at the other seven people. Doctor Dead could be anyone here. Except for me.

I must have paused too long, thinking things through, because Brutus's lizard brain decided to move things along. He grabbed my arm. "Less thinking, more action," he wittily quipped, dragging me by the arm toward the edge while I clawed at the roof's smooth surface with my free hand in a futile effort to slow him down.

"Wait!" I said, trying to delay the inevitable. "I have an idea!"

"So do I," Brutus said, looking back at me. Then a thunderclap sounded, and a bullet hole appeared in the side of his head along with the accompanying debris of the exit wound. He looked surprised for a moment, then tilted slowly over the edge with his fingers still hooked into the cloth of my shirt sleeve, dragging me along with him.

I heard an "oof!" behind me and felt someone grab my leg. I glanced down to see Lucent lying prone, holding on to me. Funny. I figured anyone with a name like *Lucent* would probably be the bad guy. Behind him, Janine stood with the smoking gun she had just pulled out of her purse. *Well*, I thought, *actual heroes trying to save someone, super or not.* Why hadn't they started by saving Gary?

Brutus, assuredly dead already, fell, and the jerk of his clenched fingers as they disentangled themselves from my plaid LL Bean shirt sleeve would certainly have pulled me off the edge if it hadn't been for Lucent's extra weight holding me back. I happened to glance up at that moment to see Joshua standing a few feet away, looking down as Brutus plunged to a redundant death. Joshua's toes were hanging over the edge as if he had no fear at all of falling. Sure, some people are born that way, but he also wore the slightest of smiles.

He caught me watching him and his smile disappeared. And then it all fit together. My speculation was correct: Doctor Dead was there with us. He knew that I knew, and there was no profit in pretending I didn't.

I rolled over toward him suddenly, breaking Lucent's grip on my legs, and slapped my hand against the back of Joshua's — Doctor Dead's — knee. His leg swung out over infinity and he fell, twisting toward me and grabbing the back of my shirt as he went.

Both of us flipped over the side. I grabbed Joshua's shirt as he held mine, and pulled him close. In my line of work at Better Hero, Inc., I'd learned that when teleporters teleported, they always took along whatever was attached to them. And by God, I was going to hang onto this asshole as though my life depended on it, at least until we were teleported onto solid ground.

There were flaws in this plan. But the biggest one was that I was apparently wrong about teleporters, and he just disappeared from my grip, leaving me with nothing but a cold, fast breeze for company and a quickly approaching pavement in my future.

I turned to face the sky and told myself, *Fly, fly, you fool! You're the one. Doctor Dead didn't lie, and you can really fly!* I stretched my arms, trying to will myself forward into the deep blue sky.

I almost believed it would happen.

I smacked into the pavement at over two hundred kilometres an hour, blood splattered all around me. Brutus was only a few feet away, with Gary and Ralph adding to the pool of gore. I was on my back, staring up at the sky, which had darkened to the shade of new Levi's blue jeans as the sun set.

I didn't move. Why would I? I was dead, covered with blood. Why was I still thinking? Was this a new useless superpower, to be able to retain consciousness after death? Weren't there horror movies written about this?

I twitched my right little finger and felt it move. I took a shallow breath, expecting that the grind of shattered ribs would destroy me. It didn't. I didn't feel dead. I hurt a lot, like someone had used me as a punching bag. Could it be?

There are several levels of invulnerability, a whole rainbow scale of how much damage you can take, from 'fairly durable' to 'impervious'. Some just flexed to absorb damage like Silly Putty, spreading out so the impact event took a millisecond longer, causing less damage overall. Maybe I was one of those. It still hurt like hell, but I'd live through it. I took another longer, deeper breath and realized that the blood and gore beneath me was not mine, but came from the three who had landed before me. My vision was blurred, presumably due to my eyes reshaping during the impact, but things were slowly coming back into focus.

I had an ability. Thirty-five years old, and I'd never suspected it. I'd call it 'not a great ability', but on the other hand, I was still alive.

There was a sudden *puff* of displaced air nearby, and I had the sense to lie still, eyes staring forward, while Doctor Dead strolled over to gloat at me, standing outside the perimeter of the pool of blood to keep his shoes clean. He smirked and snorted, then disappeared with a *pop*.

I didn't know where he went, but I was sure he'd return soon. I had to move quickly. If I could get outside the dead zone of phone reception and call my office, the rest of us might live through this. I rolled over onto my hands and knees, grunting in pain, and felt around for my phone. What was left of it was in my back pocket; it had been crushed between my body and the pavement when I landed. *Damn.*

There was a decent chance that the mess representing Brutus would have a phone among the blood-saturated clothes, and I found it. I wiped the blood off the screen with a shirttail and turned it on. And how about that, Brutus had been too dumb or too self-confident to use a PIN. On the other hand, there were still zero bars. No signal.

I stumbled into the darkness of the desert, looking for a good bar or two. I only managed to travel twenty metres or so before I heard Doctor Dead's *puff* again, and I dropped down into the sand, hoping he hadn't been facing me when he appeared. There wasn't much light, anyway; a half-moon was in the sky, casting grey shadows. I peeked over a hump in the sand and could see Joshua unfold a beach chair. There was a soft *pop* as he opened a beer.

What an ass.

He sat in the chair and looked down at the bloody mess of bodies, then back up at the building. In the dim moonlight, somehow he'd missed the fact that I was no longer lying among the pile of twisted limbs. I thought about how easy it would be for me to run up, grab him from behind, and then …

Then he'd disappear again, and I would have lost my advantage. Worse, he could transport me to a volcano and *then* disappear. I think that the only reason he hadn't done that during our first dance together was because he wanted to see all the bodies in one neat pile. Sick bastard.

I hid Brutus's phone under my coat to obscure its light and checked the bars again. Was twenty yards away from the monolith far enough to give me some signal? No, it wasn't. For all I knew, I'd have to travel kilometres to get a signal, and right now, I'd have to do it with a very slow and silent belly crawl through rocks and sand.

I was sure the five remaining on top of the building could see us both: Joshua patiently waiting for the next person to leap into oblivion, and me lying behind a low berm of sand some fifteen feet from his back.

A dark object streaked down from above and Joshua jumped excitedly out of his chair. That is to say, he teleported from a sitting to a standing position. Teleporters are lay-zee. The body—or thing—smashed into the rest of the gore just as I heard a soft whump in the sand about two metres to my right. I assumed some wildlife had just arrived to eat me since everything else was going so well.

Joshua walked over to the pile of bodies and picked up the first object: Janine's purse. It only took me a moment to surmise that the second object I'd heard wasn't wildlife and that the purse had been merely a distraction so Joshua wouldn't hear the other object land near me. I slithered over to it. It would have been hard to locate, except that part of it was glowing with a soft blue light.

I picked it up. It was Janine's gun. There was some sticky wet smudge on it, like glowing silver paint, put there so I could find it. *Lucent, I knew you had something going on besides a funky name.*

I stood up. Joshua turned and saw me at just about the same time I shot him, and kept shooting him. *Thanks, Janine.*

I stepped over to Joshua while keeping the gun trained on him. Joshua gurgled for a minute before dying. I half expected him to teleport off to a hospital, but the bullet hole in his head must have slowed him down. It was a shame that we'd never really know what drove him to do this, but teleporters rarely stuck around long enough to be interrogated.

From above, there was a shout, distorted by distance. "Did you get him?"

"Yeah," I shouted back. "I think I did." I told them that I was headed out to get a signal, and they waved and shouted back. Some glowing object drifted down toward me and I plucked it out of the air. One of them had made a parachute out of a shirt and secured a phone below it. Well, two was better than one. The glowing stuff was liberally applied so I could see it easily, and I wondered where the luminescent fluids were coming from.

Someone shouted the PIN to me. I tested it, then started walking. It took me close to three kilometres before I got a signal, and then I called my boss, Brenda, at home.

Help was sent. We would live, or half of us would anyway. While I sat and waited, I started planning on how Better Hero could market Lucent's ability, which depended somewhat on where the glowy juice was coming from. I hoped it was spit or tears. Blood was one rung further down the ladder of gross bodily fluids, just above snot, and I didn't want to go any lower than that.

Once the survivors were back together at headquarters, I returned Janine's gun to her. "You always pack a gun when you go shopping?"

She smiled and said, "I'm a cop."

"Oh," I said, and then I probably just gaped stupidly for a moment. But one question bugged me and I had to ask her, "At the risk of ruining a perfect date, I'm curious; why didn't you shoot Brutus when he was tossing Gary off the side?"

"Date, huh?" She shrugged, her mouth twisting. "I figured Doctor Dead had to be one of the people there. If I pulled my gun before I knew who it was, I'd have lost my advantage. Until Gary made that stupid threat to Brutus, I was hoping that it was all staged, that Ralph's death was fake, that this was a big joke, and that Gary could actually fly. Like, um, what was that old TV show with the hidden cameras?"

I lifted my hands like I didn't know it was *Candid Camera*. I mean, that would seriously date me.

"Anyway," Janine began, then she just kind of trailed off and sighed, like she knew she'd be explaining the same thing to a lot of other people soon.

"Well, thanks for saving me," I said, trying to put a positive slant on the mess.

"It was Lucent's idea to toss the gun to you. He put some of his blood on it so you could find it in the dark."

Just blood. I felt relieved. Better Hero could find a place for the guy somewhere. "So, would you like to —"

"No."

"No?"

"Coffee, donuts, Triscuits with mustard and shrimp, whatever you're about to say. I'm not going out with you. We went through a traumatic experience together. That's not a great start." I followed her critical gaze down to my clothing; yeah, I was still covered in crusty, drying blood.

Okay, my timing just sucked. I admit it. She knew where I worked, though, so if she changed her mind, she knew where to find me. As for me? I was impervious. Well, "fairly durable." I had a full-body bruise, but it looked like I could take a punch. Or a fall. There were already a half dozen heroes who called themselves "Fall Guy" or "The Original Fall Guy" or even "The Guy Who Would be Fall Guy if the Name Wasn't Already Taken," so I opted not to take any name at all. I suppose Better Hero might come up with a good way for me to market my ability, but they were already paying me to help others find their way. If there was some other job that required being punched hard or slammed against other objects, I wasn't interested.

If life wanted me to take risks, let it be limited to witty banter in a grocery store, Triscuits or no Triscuits. That was enough for me.

GOLDEN

Catherine Lewis

*Chinese Canadian writer **Catherine Lewis**'s debut chapbook Zipless (845 Press) is a finalist for the 2021 Bisexual Book Award for Poetry. Her work has been published in* The Humber Literary Review *and shortlisted in contests hosted by* The Fiddlehead *and* Room Magazine. *Catch her on Instagram or Twitter at @cat_writes_604 or at catherinewriter.com. 'Golden' was shortlisted for our 2022 Magpie Award for Poetry.*

Golden

A few times a year, like at Chinese New Year,
by our suburban kitchen table's temporary altar of incense, by the trays
of oranges and lucky candies cobbled together the night before,

or like on my birthday — okay, definitely on my birthday —
or always at Christmas, under our tinselled-up tree
with the paper decorations I made in my Scarborough
    kindergarten class:

Red envelopes arrive for my sister and me
on each of these occasions, with fresh banknotes
from each Grandma, from each married aunt or uncle.
A matched pair unfailingly shows up from Mom and Dad.

These envelopes are sometimes preprinted with wishes for prosperity,
in a language our parents have to translate for us all our lives.

In recent years, Mom's and Dad's arrive
bearing only their surname emblazoned in gold.

One single Chinese character
preprinted in crisp shiny thick golden text.
Sharp contrast from heavy red paper
that's sometimes shiny, sometimes matte.
Sometimes bearing a different font from the last.

When I ask Mom whether she got them custom-made,
I already know the answer.
I just know.

I just know that wherever she bought them
there are walls
       and walls
           and walls
of envelopes preprinted with the limited set of Chinese surnames
in existence.

The complete list of Chinese surnames is short.
The list of Western surnames is long.

For year after year, during my second decade of marriage
to someone not Chinese,
the red envelopes my WASP husband and I give out
at Christmas or Chinese New Year or on birthdays
                    do not carry a Chinese surname.

Just generic red envelopes my white husband and I got for free
at the mall or at the bank or with the London Drugs corporate logo,
                  not that there's anything wrong with that.

Golden

Still, they're nothing like the red envelopes my sister hands out,
with only her married Chinese surname in crisp golden text.

I hadn't realized this would be a consequence of me marrying white.

I ask, *Mom, what am I supposed to do?*
I'm not that excited about giving out the generic envelopes anymore,
I have gotten sick of using the few Hello Kitty ones I could find.

Mom says, *Well, we could get some custom-made for you.*

In Hong Kong, two days before my cousin pours tea for us
at his wedding, Mom leads our family through an underground
mini mall's corridor, to a tiny glass-walled shop

with wall after wall after wall of the few hundred most common
Chinese surnames preprinted on red, orange, yellow envelopes
in clear plastic boxes spiralling all the way up to the ceiling.

My sister and her husband tell the shopkeeper
their Chinese surname, before the man plucks out box after box.
There is, of course, a whole section for them:
some envelopes in red, some in yellow,
all of them emblazoned with golden text,
in a wide selection of different fonts.
Half a dozen different choices for my sister and her husband.

My tall, bespectacled WASP husband and I sit down
with the shopkeeper. Flip though his catalogue of sample envelopes.
Write down our custom golden text.

The shopkeeper mocks it up in Microsoft Word,
printing out a black-and-white prototype he affixes
to the same dark red matte envelopes my parents have.

We prepay the deposit for pickup.
So, in a few business days,
I can finally start living the life I always meant to have.

THE HUMMINGBIRD FLASH FICTION PRIZE

THE 2022 HUMMINGBIRD FLASH FICTION PRIZE

The 2022 Hummingbird Prize for Flash Fiction contenders landed with "nerve and verve" and were, according to final judge **Bob Thurber**, "a fine batch of stories in a variety of themes with boldness and energy. Fun to read. Engaging. Fun to consider. It was truly a delight to be absorbed by so much good writing, and to become immersed in a flood of fresh, lively prose."

Alan Sincic's 'Not What You Think' placed first and will appear in this issue. Bob described it as "daring and evocative. I found the piece, quite frankly, uncomfortably absorbing."

MJ Malleck is the runner-up with 'The Dog I Loved', which will also appear in this issue. Bob found it to be "a neat, clean, nostalgic delight. A brief reminiscence delivered with a modest reflective voice. Though subtle, the emotive movement reverberated like a chime with each subsequent reading. It repeatedly left me smiling."

We have three notable mentions this year: **Kelli Allen** for 'When a Man Knows Much More Than We Ever Did', **Elizabeth Nash** for 'Aria of the Birds', and **Alan Sincic** for 'The Painting', which are "all solid contenders with admirable qualities." Look for these stories in subsequent issues of the magazine.

Congratulations to the winners and the following shortlisted authors:

Alan Sincic, 'The Painting'
Alan Sincic, 'Not What You Think'
Cadence Mandybura, 'Nadia vs Her Feet'
Elizabeth Nash, 'Aria of the Birds'
Erin A Sayers, 'Fairy Tale'
Kelli Allen, 'When A Man Knows Much More Than We Ever Did'
MJ Malleck, 'The Dog I Loved'
Mitchell Toews, 'Luck!'
Red Charles, 'Unalone'
William Kaufmann, 'Prison Break'

Many thanks to Bob Thurber for his discerning eye and to all of this year's entrants for supporting *Pulp Literature*!

Alan Sincic is a teacher at Valencia College. His fiction appears in Boulevard Online, New Ohio Review, Greensboro Review, The Saturday Evening Post, Big Fiction, Master's Review, Grist, *and elsewhere. His short stories have won contests sponsored by* The Texas Observer, Hunger Mountain, Driftwood Press, The Prism Review, *and others. After earning an MA in Literature at the University of Florida and a poetry fellowship at Columbia, Alan earned his MFA at Western New England University. Last year the opening chapter of his novel* The Slapjack *won the 2021 First Pages Prize. His story 'Blind Maggie' won our 2021 Bumblebee Flash Fiction Contest. Visit him at alansincic.com.*

MJ Malleck studied journalism and spent decades crafting corporate communications while winning bouts of two truths and a lie. Her fiction has recently appeared in Agnes & True, The Temz Review, *and* EVENT.

Not What You Think

by Alan Sincic

This book is not what you think it is. It does not begin with you sitting in the hollow of a tree, eating crackers and scratching your elbow as you look out across the forest in the morning. Ignore that picture over there. That was a mistake.

In fact, you shouldn't even be reading this sentence, this sentence that talks about how you left home to live by yourself in the middle of the woods, in this treehouse you carved out of the hollow of the tree, with the table and the chairs and the stairs, with the wooden bedroom with the wooden lamp, the wooden rug, the wooden bed, and the pair of wooden shoes. You would not be doing something like that. That does not sound like you at all. Better we just end the story here.

Even now it's not too late to turn back. You could close the book here, at this word, *here,* before the bear comes to visit. Because once the bear comes to visit, everything changes. That's it. That's just the way it goes when the bear comes to visit. You have to hide up in the branches at the top of the tree, with your toast and blackberry jam and your funny papers and your pyjama bottoms flapping in the breeze, while the bear (who knows better than to crack a book), he totters round the kitchen with his big paws a-clackin' across the beautiful tablecloth you finished carving the night before.

Now you're stuck. If you throw the bottle of jam at the bear, he's liable to get mad and come after you. If you climb down to offer the bear some jam, there's not going to be enough jam for you. But if you just sit up here in the branches waiting for something to happen, then nothing is going to happen.

Which might be nice for a change, right? Nothing happens. Good luck with that one. The problem with *nothing happens* is that it never happens that way. It's never nothing happens. Something always happens.

The branch breaks. Or the bear leaves. Or the bear so loves the house he — maybe should he stay? Other bears will come to visit when they hear about what a good time this bear is having, bear after bear crawling in through your windows and over your crockery and across your newly waxed wooden floor. In any case, and no matter what happens, your oatmeal's getting cold.

There's the sound of thunder overhead. The wind picks up. Looks like it's gonna rain.

Up and down the leaves around you buoy. Up and down you ride the branch. It's the weight of the bears, shuffling round the house in the hollow of the tree, thumping round the kitchen and the parlour, nosing up under the bed and the sofa, sniffing at the sill of the window you scrambled out a second ago.

On the lookout, they are, for a something they none of them seen before. What would it be? Hard to say. Something like enough of a bear to fit a bear, but fresh enough to be a sign of something other. Other. That would be you. Out the window, a snout. A sniff. A nose, the black nose, the wet-as-a-pebble nose of a bear.

Below you, on the ground, in a cradle of root and leaf and random tinder, lies the book. The wind nibbles at the open page, the yellow bond brittle at the edges from all the seasons of wear. *Turn the page*, you're thinking, *turn it back*, but that would be the wrong direction, the wrong position, upwind of the bears. No, not a place to be. Such a random thing, the wind, to carry the scent of you hither and thither.

And then you notice it, and *wow* you think. Not *wow* the bears. We know about the bears. The *wow* is for the woods. What with the fog and all, the clunk of the jar, the bother with the comics, how to fold them under the arm in the course of climbing the tree, you forgot about the woods. How big and how broad. In a roll up and down the hills, nothing but trees in every direction.

Something. You sniff the air. From a ways. Over yonder. Far. A whiff of smoke. Brick of a chimney. Human, the smell.

The jar skitters off the branch and somersaults into the turf. Thump. The wind hits the funnies, smacks them open, kites them away. The toast, it flippers up to follow, but a crow swoops. Snatches. Up into the cloud of the leaf and the branch in the blue it goes. Gone the funnies. Gone the toast and the butter and the crisp of the morning, out, out over the yonder and away.

Overhead, the clouds they blossom. The branch quivers with a burden. You shift your weight inward, to where the branch and the trunk converge.

It rises up around you—the scent of the oak, the sap, the bark, and the sod, the lichen and the humus and the scat and the fur and the snap of the tinder. With your hind legs you grip the trunk and downward you slide. How the bark it crackles. How the wind it sings. And here the jar. And here the scent of the berry. Click-clack the claw on the tin of the lid. You shoulder your brother aside. You lap at the sweetness. You paw at the husk of the leather, here in the hollow of the root. You tear the bud open. The yellow petals you shatter.

From heaven a growl. A gift of rain. From deep in the heart of the animate earth, up from the hollow in the heart of you, a growl in return. You shed the rain, you all of you, with a bristle and a shake, and into the green cover you amble, and onto the trail to carry you home.

Four awards for genre-busting fiction and poetry

The Bumblebee Flash Fiction Contest

Deadline: 15 February

Prize: $300

The Magpie Award for Poetry

Deadline: 15 April
First Prize: $500

The Hummingbird Flash Fiction Prize

Deadline: 15 June
Prize: $300

The Raven Short Story Contest

Deadline: 15 October
Prize: $300

For more information visit: pulpliterature.com/contests

Short stories, poetry, and comics you can't put down.

The Dog I Loved

BY MJ MALLECK

Our one-bathroom backsplit was jam-packed with a strict mother, up to seven kids, a hairy and drooly lab–shepherd mutt, and, when the older kids moved out, a paying boarder too. If you were to enter through the front door, which you could only do if you were company and it was Christmas, you would find a room too precious to play in. A couch and two matching chairs that would never feel denim against their golden brocade. Heavy forest-green drapes flanking a plate-glass window, where I thought I'd win at hide-and-seek. Left alone too long in the forbidden room, I scratched at the tiny bits of glass sparkling my bare arms and gave myself a tattle-tale rash.

The dog I loved was not the mutt, that slobbery, tail-thumping dog that invited petting even when he was eating kibble. The dog I loved was eight inches high and twelve inches long.

Once I was eight, it became my job on Saturdays to dust the front room. Before she graduated to hanging wet sheets on the line, my older sister trained me. She showed me how to lay a clean tea towel on the couch and to 'very gently' place upon it the Blue Mountain ashtray, the pinwheel crystal rosebud vase, the heavy purple glass grapes with silk leaves and tendrils, and the porcelain dog. My sister, spraying Windex for the last time onto the glass-covered coffee table, was immune to the dog. My sister was most concerned to teach me to (a) not break anything and (b) put everything back in its exact place.

The dog I loved stood on the farthest end of the table, so I dusted her last and held her the longest. I felt the smooth ridges of her caramel-and-white mane as I groomed her with the dust cloth. I kissed the cool blackness of her nose and rubbed the delicate bone of her shins. I played shake-a-paw with her.

Later, when a pink swan candy dish appeared, my dog was moved to a spot on the carpet underneath the coffee table. She stood solidly on three legs, her right paw lifted beneath her slender, pointing nose. She was not guarding anything in place; she was trying to get my attention. She was a smart dog, like Lassie, and she was about to bark and twirl around and have me follow her to save someone who lived an interesting life outside my front door.

A COLD PLACE BETWEEN THE SHORES

Mikael Lopez & Artyom Trakhanov

Mikael Lopez *is a Swedish writer whose work has been published in various anthologies. His first graphic novel,* Berzerkid *(a collaboration with artist Gax), was published by Peow in 2021. Mikael's graphic short 'Forgive My Delay' appeared in* Pulp Literature *Issue 36, Autumn 2022.*

Artyom Trakhanov *is a notorious Slavic nihilist, dedicated to creating comics in two genres: folk horror and sci-fi eco-thrillers. His work appears in* Undertow, Turncoat, The 7 Deadly Sins, First Knife, *and elsewhere.*

A COLD PLACE BETWEEN THE SHORES

story
Mikael Lopez

art
Artyom Trakhanov

The border between Finland and Silva Ursa, 2044.

Lieutenant Autio, commander of 17th Platoon.

I am Mesi.
I speak for my family...

...The Nameless of Silva Ursa.
One of you has ended the life of our brother, and so we must have retribution...
...or you will have war.

We do not want war.
The border agreement has always been respected by both sides, and we've never had an incident before.
Is all this really necessary?
Was this necessary?
What do you want?
Bring me the one, the one who did this.
The one will tell me why this happened.
Järviranta.

You are the one?
Yes.
Why?
GULP
It was an accident.
I saw a shape out on the ice, but it was too dark to see clearly.
I didn't want to raise a false alarm, so I went to see if there really was something out there.
He just—
He came from out of nowhere, climbed out of a hole in the ice. I just reacted, didn't think.
I shot him.
Every member of our family is precious to us, vital for our survival.
Each death is a profound loss for those of us who still breathe.
Now one of our sisters has lost a mate...
...and I have lost a son.
But you will take my son's place and join our family, and we will slowly forget our sorrow.
Or there will be a war.

...
I'll go with you.
What? You can't—
Good.
Järviranta, you don't have to do this.
I know, sir. But I want to.
It's like you always say, "carry the burden of your errors."
Goodbye, sir.

THE END

PRETTY LIES: BLOW THIS CANDLE OUT

Mel Anastasiou

Mel Anastasiou is a novel acquisitions and story editor with Pulp Literature Press, and she co-founded Pulp Literature magazine in 2013. Mel helps writers develop through her structural editing, the popular 'Writing Muse' Twitter feed, and two workbooks, The Writer's Boon Companion: Thirty Days Towards an Extraordinary Volume and The Writer's Friend and Confidante: Thirty Days of Narrative Achievement. Her fiction includes the Hertfordshire Pub Mysteries, the Monument Studio Mysteries, and the Stella Ryman Mysteries, for which she won a Literary Titan Gold book award and was longlisted for the Leacock Medal.

Blow this Candle Out

It's the golden summer of 1974 in Bowen Island, BC. Inspired by the story of Orpheus and Eurydice, Jenny Riley tries to bring her dead boyfriend Joey back from the ghost world, but gives him up when he proves intent instead upon bringing her into the ghost world to stay. Malcolm, Adrian, and Chief Layton are all walking razors' edges as Moira drags Jenny into her own perilous agenda for life after death. Here is the final section of Pretty Lies: A Ghost Story.

Chapter 26

Chief Layton had trained most of the young fellows directing the cars on the bottom deck of the ferry, and there was nothing more he could tell them. He propped himself against the Sunshine Deck bulkhead and reflected that responsibility without control over outcomes had long been the curse of his professional and personal lives.

Foot passengers clanged up the metal steps towards him, passed him by, and walked out into the sunshine. Nobody asked him whether he was ill; a man in uniform was expected to take care of them, not the other way around. He closed his eyes and waited for the pain to come again.

Two hands took him by the shoulders, and a young man's voice spoke urgently.

"Sir. Sir! Open your eyes, please."

The hands dropped away, and Chief Layton opened his eyes. Staring back at him was the Chinese fellow who'd brought the injured child on board the ferry earlier that day.

Chief said, "The purser is trained in first aid." As expected, his pain deepened and travelled outwards from his centre like light from the Christmas star.

"I don't need first aid," the young man answered. I need somebody to look at my tongue." He clicked his tongue and brought his face up close to Chief's. "I might have taken an orange pill. I was on a bus, and I lost track of the drug in my pocket. I never take drugs, though. Maybe I fell asleep. Maybe I dreamed the young bus driver. What do you think?"

Chief Layton thought about his wife, dead ten years; and maybe ten years without her was enough. With this thought, his pain vanished. By now he was so tired he had to hold on to the young fellow to keep upright. "What's your name?"

"Malcolm."

"Malcolm, take a minute. You young people don't know what trouble is." He slid down the metal bulkhead to sit on the deck floor. Malcolm sat down at his side. He was in his twenties, far too old to be trembling like a child. Or else far too young to shake like an old man. But drugs would do that to a person.

Malcolm asked, "Are you all right, sir? You don't look well to me."

"Are you a doctor?"

"Not yet. I'd better go get that purser guy."

"Wait." The pain was gone. If he reported it to the captain or the purser, there would be more pressure to retire, and then what would Chief Layton do with his time on earth? Competence in your field had to go somewhere. "Give it a little time, will you?"

Malcolm stood up and moved to the rail. "What *is* that?"

"What is what?"

"Something is heading right for the ferryboat. We're going to crash."

"We're hardly out of port. It seems unlikely." Chief Layton struggled to get to his feet, but the stabbing feeling in his chest returned and sat him down again. He groaned under his breath. "You'd better be sure you're not giving false alarms, young man. Did you say you took drugs?"

"No. Please, look at the water. It's like black waves coming out of nowhere and heading for us."

"Calm down. We're in a sheltered area."

Malcolm continued, "If you could just take a ruler and draw along it, the line of rough water points right at us."

Chief Layton closed his eyes. Responsibility without control. "Find the captain, then. Sound the alarm."

But it was as if Malcolm didn't hear him. "It's getting closer. It'll be here in a minute."

Finally, Chief Layton got to his feet and looked.

Chapter 27

Moira believed that in this modern life, with its streetcars, radios, and electric irons, only trouble came free of charge. Furthermore, she'd paid Jenny plenty in effort, even though there was little to show for it except the girl's handsome, lying boyfriend dead in the seat of a broken automobile.

Moira had done her best for Jenny, and she was perfectly satisfied to have her friend where she wanted her, balanced on the rail of a great white ship and holding on with both hands to the upright support. Moira clung to her own upright and grinned at Jenny, who was not exactly a goddess of good sense and wisdom but at least held on tight while the black waves tossed the vessel like a bit of paper dropped on the surface. Like a candy wrapper a kid had chucked into the water.

Black skies boiled, and then opened to let the sun shine through. The rain thrashed back across the sky and drenched them. Jenny shouted something, but even though the two were standing only a few feet apart on the rail, the wind snatched her words out of the air and blew them away from the ship. Moira leaned closer to hear, and a sudden and illogical break in the storm turned the sky from black to blue and the sea from silver to green. The raging noises retreated, and she made out Jenny's words.

"I want to go back."

"Back to the car crash? Back to your Joe?"

"Not to him! Never again."

Moira hid her amusement at Jenny's fierce denial. Nobody altered their affections on a dime, however badly a fellow treated them. But the last thing a broken heart like Jenny's wanted to hear was the truth, so Moira only said, "Never say never."

"Let me go home. That's all I want."

"What you want?" Moira snorted, and the sky turned black and stormy as before. "It's been all about *what you want* for some time now. Wouldn't you agree?"

Jenny seemed hardly to have heard. She stared down the side of the ship.

Moira snapped, "Don't look down. Look at me."

Jenny did. The skies poured rain at a hard angle, and Moira had to raise her voice again to be heard.

"Haven't I been a friend to the end?" Moira wanted to hold her hands out wide, but she'd be crazy to let go of the upright. "Except for when I pretended to drown you—"

"Pretended? You nearly killed me."

Moira huffed. "I was play-acting. Anybody with a mind would know. Look at the facts, sister. Haven't I helped you at every turn of the road?"

Scowling, Jenny answered, "Yes. But—"

"Then help me get Philip back. He's on this boat somewhere. I want him to darned well admire me like he did before. I want him to appreciate my spirit, my looks, my adventurous heart. When he sees me up on this rail, he'll remember how he loves me. And then he'll marry me and we'll happily-ever-after."

Jenny peered at her through the rain, disbelief plain in the slant of her eyebrows. "Moira, nothing's that simple."

"True love is."

"It's not true love if it's only one person doing the loving."

"Says you," Moira retorted.

"Just consider the possibility that you won't get your happily-ever-after with Philip. Maybe you need to work on making a different future for yourself."

"What a laugh that piece of advice is, coming from you, with your dead boyfriend."

"Maybe you should think about ... an alternate future."

Jenny appeared to be choosing her words with care, and Moira hated every one of them. She was glad of the interruption when a wash of water picked up an ashtray from an iron stand on the deck and bounced it against the rail below her.

Moira said, "Let's change the subject, chum. I love a good rainstorm. Makes a person glad to be alive, I think."

"Sure. Sure it does. For those of us who are alive, anyway." Jenny glanced down at the streaming deck, and for a moment Moira feared she'd climb down off the rail. Instead, Jenny held up her hand, preparatory to making a point. The gesture was that of an orator, or a lying politician. She said, "Look, Moira, I understand your romantic scenario. It even makes a certain amount of sense to show off for a man, if he's the type that likes that kind of mind game. But Moira, I have to ask you, and this is important —"

"Just a minute, will you? Hold on tight." Moira pushed her hair out of her eyes. The sun reappeared from behind black clouds, vanished, and another wave washed across the deck. This time the ship's pitch was so extreme that the ashtray hit the nearest bulkhead, bucked over the rail, and fell into the roiling sea below. "You're jinxing it. I think you're talking too much."

"I haven't said enough." Jenny gripped her upright with both hands and leaned closer to Moira. "Answer me this. Why here? Why on the side rail of this bloody boat? Can't you think of something marginally less dangerous and a lot more glamorous?"

"Isn't it obvious? This is where I met him."

"On a boat rail? How romantic."

Moira tossed her head. "More romantic than a car crash, chum."

"Touché. Really touché."

Brave words. There could be no better friend than a valiant woman. Moira had chosen well.

She said, "I was up on the rail showing off, just like this, and I caught his eye and waved. He smiled. He came right to me. So he is the type you mentioned."

"And handsome as hell, I bet." Jenny shook her head. "Then what happened?"

Moira was about to tell her when the boat shifted under them, and it was all she could do to keep her feet. She checked that Jenny was still hanging on and safely vertical. "Then Philip and I fell in love. See, I don't give up."

"Really? I hadn't noticed."

"Sarcasm is the cheapest form of humour, sister. Listen to me when I tell you, I don't give up because love doesn't give up."

"I think it does, actually."

"Not mine. I'm true."

"What is truth?" Jenny asked. "Define truth."

"For cat's sake, don't be such a professor. Listen, if I try to jump and Philip rescues me, then I'll be in his arms, pale and grateful."

Jenny laughed. "You?"

"I can be pale and grateful when it counts. The important thing is that I jump and Philip saves me."

"How do you know Philip will save you?"

"Because he loves me. And anyway, he works on the boat. Saving people is his responsibility."

Jenny nodded, and her wet hair fell forward over her face. "Then why in blazes do you need me here?"

"Because you're my friend.'

"I can be your friend from a safe distance. I can be your friend from my own home."

"I don't need a pen friend, sister. I need you here on the spot. To attract his attention, for one thing."

"And exactly how would you like me to do that? Wave at him? Shout, Philip, look at this fearless woman? Like a ringmaster at the circus?"

"Sure, you can wave. And once he sees you, you act admiring of me."

"I thought Philip was supposed to admire you."

"Oh, be yourself." Did Jenny know nothing of men? "You have to act all complimentary to show him I'm not some lonely sad dame but a lovely young woman who adores to laugh and be daring. Somebody everybody wants to act like and be with. That's your job. And he will rescue me, and I can get to work on becoming his wife and the mother of his children. That part I can do on my own."

Jenny gazed at her with unnecessarily sad eyes. "Right. Did you really jump off this boat before?"

"Yes, of course."

"I'll bet that's how you d—"

Moira talked over her. "I've tried again and again to get his attention. I've jumped a thousand times. He never rescues me."

"A thousand times. You're stuck, aren't you? Oh, god, Moira, I'm so sorry."

Jenny did look sorry, sorrier than Moira considered appropriate just when success was within reach. She'd be darned if she was going to accept anybody's pity when everything was going so well. "Chin up, sister, because now *you're* here. You know what it means to be stuck, and I know what we both need to do to unstick me."

"But what if I get stuck with you?"

Clouds gathered and dropped rain in sheets. Jenny looked down the side of the ship, precisely as Moira had warned her not to, and nearly lost her balance. She pivoted to regain her footing and glanced up at the Sunshine Deck. "There's somebody up there."

"Who? Is it Philip?" Moira craned her neck to see. At the rail of the deck above them stood two men, braced against the weather and engaged in furious discussion. Even through the rain, one of them was more familiar to her than the palm of her own hand. "There he is. Holy Moses, there's Philip at last."

"No, it's …"

Moira's heart was buoyant as a cork on the surface of the sea. "I knew it, Jenny. I was sure my situation would change if you'd just finally, unselfishly, act like a good pal. Get ready to admire me. Get ready to jump."

Jenny looked up through the downpour. "That's not Philip. That's my, well, my friend Malcolm. And the old man is—"

"There's no old man." Moira smiled through wet hair that hung in rat's tails around her face. So much in life was uncertain, even inexplicable, but she knew her sweetheart when she saw him. "A handsome young man in uniform shouldn't be too hard for you to spot. Look again, chum. But don't be too obvious about it. And think about this: if necessary, the waves will cushion our fall."

Chapter 28

What if he spooked her? The thought nailed Malcolm to the deck. He hung on to the old chief and gaped down at the railing below like some kind of fool. He saw the line of Jenny's thigh stretch and her shorts pull tight across her rear end as she teetered on the rail, both hands on the upright. Even if he startled her, he had to do something to help.

"Do you *want* to fall overboard?" Malcolm shouted at Jenny. "Get down from there."

Jenny didn't answer. She didn't look back at him, or get down. He would have to save her after all, and the other young woman beside her on the rail as well. He told himself to take one at a time. Save one first and go back for the other. That was the logical way.

But what about the old man? He couldn't leave him here, not alone in the middle of a possible heart attack.

Night fell again and, with it, more rain. "Damn it all, make up your mind," Malcolm shouted at the sea and the sky.

Jenny kept her toehold on the wet rail and hung on to the upright. She glanced down the side of the ship. It was a killing drop to a rain-hammered, gale-tossed sea. Jenny knew perfectly well that the waves wouldn't *cushion her fall*, as Moira had put it. From this height, the waves would be the equivalent of so much unforgiving concrete.

She glanced up at the upper deck rail. Malcolm had moved out of sight; Chief Layton stood alone above them with his eyes shut, gnarled hands gripping the rail. He looked like death. Old death—not the young kind like Joey's.

A colossal wave shook the ship. She tightened her grip on the upright pole and looked up again to see Malcolm reappear at the Sunshine Deck railing. He set the old man on his feet and held him steady.

Moira, an arm's length away, reached along the rail and pinched Jenny's wrist. "Stop staring at Philip. I don't want to seem too eager. Don't you know that it's the kiss of death to male attraction?

We're doing this daring deed because we get a kick out of being bold and audacious women. Like the beauties who race cars and fly planes. Everybody knows they're the toast of high society." Moira held onto her upright and leaned closer to shout. "Jumping off a boat takes guts, glamour, and skill. We can do it."

"You'll kill both of us. And what if your Philip doesn't see, or doesn't care?"

"Then I'll do it again until he does."

Jenny imagined Moira falling down the side of the boat again and again, perishing and reanimating in an endless tumble of hope and disappointment. She might repeat her death forever, and on the day silver spaceships took humanity to the stars, Moira would stay behind, a lonely ghost on an abandoned planet, taking leaps of faith off the side of this ship and dying throughout eternity in her own endless and circular mistake.

Worse still, what if Jenny were to jump in the ghost world and die in the real world? She imagined her arms and legs flailing, fighting gravity to dive straight down as she contested an irreversible fatal decision. To break her body on the waves … how much would that hurt?

Not at all, Jenny guessed. She would not feel the impact at all.

But was there another choice on the menu?

Jenny couldn't see one. But Moira had pulled her out of the shattered Zed. Without Moira, Jenny might very well have remained with Joey, crashing over and over again. Watching him die. Jenny owed Moira for pulling her out of that other spinning, hateful destiny.

Do not distress yourself with dark imaginings. It was a little late for that advice.

Jenny jerked her chin towards the old ferry officer at the

Sunshine Deck rail. "Look up, and look carefully, Moira. He's handsome, I'll give you that, but like Cary Grant is handsome in his sixties, with white hair and good bones."

"You are loony as always, pal. Cary Grant is barely thirty." Moira peered upwards through the rain. "It's the sky's reflection on his dark hair that makes it look white."

Jenny took heart at the note of uncertainty in Moira's tone.

"Look at the man himself and not at your memories, Moira. What do you see?"

Moira stared up at Chief Layton, standing at the rail in Malcolm's supporting arms. Her smile faltered, her hand slipped on the upright, and she turned to Jenny. "It's Philip. Not another word until you agree."

Jenny grimaced. Chief Layton could not by any stretch of her imagination be mistaken for a young man. But this was not the moment to stop lying. She said, "I agree. It's Philip."

"Good," Moira said fiercely. "But why does he look like that?"

"Nobody wants to get old, Moira." Everybody wished to go on living forever. And at this, Jenny supposed, Moira was succeeding, without benefit or joy.

"What if you let Philip go?"

With obvious reluctance, Moira looked Jenny in the eye. "If I let him go, I'd lose my future. Where would I find another fellow as lovely as Philip? How could I make somebody else love me forever? It's impossible."

Moira was dead, but she was correct.

Jenny said, "Moira, you're right. You're not going to find another fellow."

"I'm pretty enough." Moira slashed at the rattail hair in front of her face and scowled.

"Sure, you're pretty. But you died young. And I think you died when you jumped from a ship like this."

"You're nuts." Moira looked down at the pounding waves. "You always think everyone's dead, my friend. You said *you* were dead in that yellow car, and here you are. You told me your Joey was dead, but I saw him, bleeding in the car. Now you say *I'm* dead. If everybody's dead, kiddo, then what's the doggone difference? And you still haven't answered my question."

"What question?"

"If I let go of loving Philip, where exactly do you think I'm going to find another fellow?"

Jenny nearly said, *Why do you need a fellow so badly? Don't you know you can live a good life on your own terms?* But maybe that was Jenny's answer. Moira required one of her own.

Moira hooked strong fingers around Jenny's arm. "Where will I find another man?"

Footsteps tapped against the deck. A voice Jenny knew as well as her own said, "Right here."

Jenny swung round on the railing and gazed down at Joey. He didn't look back at her but gave Moira his heavy-lidded, heart-stopping smile. He said, "Moira, come down here with me."

Moira clung to the rail with both hands. "With you, average Joe? Certainly not."

Joey grinned. "Hard to get."

"Fresh as several fish," Moira returned.

Joey held Moira's gaze and clasped Jenny around the waist. He pulled her down with the unfeeling strength and authority a man would bring to removing luggage from an upper shelf. He dropped her into a puddle on the deck and swung himself up onto the rail in Jenny's place. He took hold of the upright.

He said, "Look at you, Moira girl, standing on the rail like Venus right out of the ocean."

"Welcome to my clam shell." Moira held out a hand to Joey. "You are a smooth one for an average Joe. Unless Jenny minds? I'd never poach a fellow from a friend."

"Why would she care? We're history. Didn't she tell you?" Joey clasped hands with Moira. He looked down and straight at Jenny for the first time. He gave her his heartbreaker of a smile. "In every possible way, Jenny and I are history."

Jenny got to her feet and seized his ankle.

"Don't do it, Joey," she said. Don't you dare."

"Let go," Joey said. "It's time."

Jenny stood up and caught him around the knees. His blue jeans rasped against her cheek. The boat heaved against a wave, and she was down on the deck again, looking up at the two of them on the rail.

Joey shot Jenny a warning look and turned his back on her. She struggled back to her feet.

"Double dare, Moira." Joey held Moira upright with his left arm across her back and balanced the two of them on the ferry rail with his right hand on the upright. "We're double daredevils, aren't we?"

"Yes." Moira sent Jenny a triumphant look. "I told you, didn't I? Whoever watches will feel admiration."

Joey laughed. "I feel admiration."

Jenny didn't. She felt sliced to her red centre. It occurred to her that she had only a second to react.

Only a second if she didn't want to be left behind.

Less than a second, now, if she ever wanted to see Joey again.

And now, just the blink of an eye, for Moira and Joey teetered together on the rail.

Jenny moved to stop them. From behind her, Malcolm said, "Not a chance, Jenny."

She struggled against his arms towards the couple on the rail and managed only a step in their direction before Malcolm pulled her back.

Like dancers, like lovers, Joey and Moira locked hands and stepped over the side of the ship. Jenny broke free of Malcolm's grip. She ran to the rail and leaned out.

She saw Moira and Joey fall, pale as paper, into the sea.

One splash, a second splash.

And a third.

Jenny heard the cry from her left far down the rail of the boat: *"Man overboard."*

CHAPTER 29

Jenny pushed her way into the crowd of ferry passengers massing at the rail. She had to peer over and through their craning heads to see that the ferry had stopped about halfway to Bowen in order to rescue the unknown jumper.

"Is the ferry supposed to be facing the land like that?" somebody asked.

"It's a *rescue,*" somebody else answered.

"There's a streak of blood down the side of the boat." A boy in a yellow shirt hung over the rail by the empty lifeboat hook and pointed.

"That's just rust, kid," a man told him.

Jenny glanced at the kid's yellow shirt, grubby as a dog's chew toy, and at the uncombed hair above it. This was one of

Malcolm's campers. Or one of Adrian's? The kid's name was Flash, she recalled, and she ought to ask him what he was doing on this ferry alone. Instead, she turned herself sideways, wedged herself through the roil of ferry passengers, and achieved a position a little closer to the rail.

Somebody said, "They've lowered the rescue boat."

Somebody else asked, "Can you see him in the water?"

Jenny couldn't.

"It's not a man, it's a woman."

"It's a child," a passenger at the rail said.

"You're crazy. It's not a kid. He just looks small from up here."

Jenny thrust her way to the rail at last. She scanned the waves for the jumper. The woman jammed in next to her pointed out the rescue boat that manoeuvred its way along the ferryboat's side.

Jenny felt a tug at the hem of her shorts and looked down to see a small boy all dressed in blue. He wore a cap, the bill of which made it difficult to see his face properly.

He asked, "What happened to the man who jumped?"

"He's being rescued," Jenny said. "I guess they'll put him back on board. Let's hope he's okay."

"What a big show-off," the boy in blue said. "Grown-ups are stupid. They tell you what not to do, and then they do it."

"You're on the money, kid." Jenny looked at him. She saw the freckles on his forearm, and her breath caught in her throat.

She knew the pattern of those freckles the way one of her classmates had known the constellations. She and Joey had traced those arm freckles with a ballpoint pen when they were little and at particularly loose ends. Joey's freckles made a cannon, and the freckles on her own arm made a crown.

Jenny dropped to her knees in front of him. Seeing Joey now as the little boy who'd been her friend of the heart when she was a little girl broke her anger like a stick of hard candy. You could forgive a child for anything. Any misjudgement, any cruelty. Any lie.

She said, "You jumped. I thought I'd never see you again."

"I forgot to tell you something." He held one hand behind his back.

Around them, the crowd heaved and cheered. A man grunted, "They've caught the guy. Just like landing a big fish."

"Is he dead?"

"It's a girl—look at her blonde hair."

"You're blind, it's a guy."

Jenny was afraid that if she turned away to watch the rescue, the child Joey would vanish without telling her what he forgot. She moved closer to him to protect him from the push of knees around them. To keep him from leaving.

Joey's breath smelled like cola. "Here."

He brought his hand out from behind his back and held out a glass. A green glass full of something dark. Something sweet.

"What a bad potion this is," the child Joey said.

A hollow feeling grew inside her.

"Why did you drug my drink, Joey?" After his lies at the crash scene in the ghost world, she no longer expected the truth from him, but she asked anyway. Nobody lied all the time.

Joey shrugged. "I thought it was funny. Get the prude drunk. That's why."

She looked down into the darkness of the glass and saw a face reflected there, but not her face. Somebody's face, a pale shape in a car window. Tears filled her eyes, and she wiped them away.

"Don't cry, Jenny. I'm sorry I gave you that drink, and I'm sorry I pretended you were dead in the car. Dead like I am." The little boy put his hand in hers. "I just was so tired of being dead alone. I like you to do the things that I do. Like when we were kids. And at Lerner's parties."

She followed his gaze back to the green glass. It sloshed with the motion of the ferryboat on the rails but didn't spill.

"If I drink this, will you stop feeling alone?" she asked him.

His forehead wrinkled above his perfect young nose. He said, "I don't know."

"I don't want to hate you anymore. I feel better when I love you."

The child Joey touched one finger to the glass.

Jenny saw in her memory the small girl following the small boy, running to catch up, a red flower dropping from her hand as she reached out to hang on to him. Hang on tight and never let go. They were running hard to reach a corner, but she didn't remember what was around it. And it didn't matter what was around the corner as long as they were hand in hand.

She raised the glass. The cold rim touched her lips.

The little boy sighed. Before she could stop him, he took the glass back and set it to his rosebud mouth. In a practised manner, he drained it. He bent down and set the glass on the deck, where a foot kicked it over. It rolled out of sight in the crowd.

He said, "Well, that's that. Moira's waiting, I'd better go."

When he stood up, it was to his full height at twenty-two, looking down at her out of those heavy-lidded eyes. And now she saw that she'd been wrong—he hadn't appeared to her as a child to wring forgiveness from her. He'd appeared as a child because that Joey was still hers. This adult Joey didn't reach for her or meet her eyes. Even right in front of her, jostled against her breast by the crowd, he seemed as cool and distant as the bottom of the sea. No, this Joey wasn't hers any longer. He'd joined Moira.

He said, "I have to tell you something else."

"Where is she?" Jenny peered through the crowd on all sides. "Moira's not right for you. She's shallow and reckless and——"

"Stop talking. Listen. Jenny, don't come find me."

He stepped back into the crowd. She moved to follow, but a group of ferry workers hurried between them and she lost sight of him in the crowd.

Don't come find me. Joey wasn't hers anymore.

The ferryboat trembled back to life and power, and the bow swung slowly round to continue its journey towards Bowen Island and the end of the ride.

Chapter 30

The three campers found the weird orange candies in the upstairs lounge a few minutes into the second ferry trip, after Frances paid their fares at the snack bar so they could stay on board while she looked for Jenny.

The boys found the candies together because they were always together, like sticky fingers——Ketchup, Tanaka, Flash, and Two-Can Sam. But now that Ketchup was dead——no, just in hospital, numbskull!——there were three of them. Together forever. And they weren't letting anybody else in the group.

"Nobody." Two-Can was so bossy, he was like Hitler's sister. "Ketchup's in when he gets back, though."

"Okay, man," Flash agreed.

"How about Lenny?" Tanaka asked. "What about Anik?"

"Not even the Jacksons can get in the club. Olivia Newton-John, though ..." Two-Can put in. He was larger than the others, and older, and he knew some stuff, some of it pretty dirty. A good man to have around, that was Tanaka's opinion, although it was kind of a strain to keep up. "How long do we go back and forth on this stupid ferry?"

"Until Frances finds Jenny with the key to her shit Galaxie." Flash punched Two-Can and flung himself into the shadowy area between the cigarette machine and the women's toilet. "Let's sit over here."

Tanaka, Two-Can, and Flash settled their backs against the wall. The passenger lounge wasn't crowded today, but the knees boogied by them as they always did. Adult knees meant nothing to Tanaka.

Two-Can climbed up on a chair and pressed his nose to the window that looked out on the deck. "Hey, get a load of this." He pointed with his middle finger at something outside the window. Pointing with the middle finger was their new thing. "There goes that Jenny girl."

"Sittin' in her rockin' chair," Flash said. "Eatin' up her underwear."

"Flew like a little *bird*." Tanaka shivered and smacked Flash on the side of the head. Flash hit him back.

"They stopped the boat," Two-Can said. "We're just floating."

"Hey, you guys." Flash punched Tanaka, and he rubbed his arm. "You dingbats. What's that over there?"

Tanaka leaned down to look. Something orange. "Candy."

Two-Can jumped down from the seat and picked several of the candies up off the grimy floor. He held them out to the others on the palm of his hand. They were crazy thin, stuck to waxed paper, and they looked like a breath would blow them away.

Something new in the world of candy.

"They're too dirty to eat," Tanaka said.

"Are you my mother?" Two-Can squeezed down at Tanaka's side. "Anyway, what do you care? They're mine."

"I saw them first," Flash pointed out.

"They're all of ours." Tanaka batted at Two-Can's hand, but the fist closed tight. Treasure was rare, and there were rules. "Normally I don't eat stuff from the ground, though."

"I'll take yours." Flash rolled across Two-Can's lap and wiggled his arm and shoulder under the cigarette machine. He squirmed back with several more of the same candies in his hand. Tanaka couldn't see how many.

Tanaka put his cheek against the carpet and scanned the area under the cigarette machine, as well as the crevice formed by the metal lip at the bottom of the washroom door. Everyone always forgot to check there. He nodded to himself and pulled up a strip of five candies. "I'm just saying we should wash them."

"Wimp."

"Jam tart. Anyway, they're so thin, they'd melt off the paper. What's all the shouting about outside? Ferryboats aren't supposed to stop in the middle of the water." Flash peered out the window and shrugged.

"Honey, you can't eat one." Tanaka slouched lower against the wall, lifted up his shirt, tore off one of the orange candies, and nestled it in his belly button.

Two-Can laughed. "Ooh, sexy."

Tanaka felt a small balloon of satisfaction rise inside him.

"Honey you can't eat two." Two-Can put a candy on each of his eyelids and lay down dead on the lounge carpet.

"Honey, you can't eat five." Tanaka twisted his lip upwards and

his nose downwards. He could only hold one candy there, so he shoved the other two into his nostrils. He laughed himself sideways, and the candies shot out of his nose and went flying. To get them back, he had to crawl under the seats, but before he could get his hands on the candies, Two-Can scooped them up.

"Divide them. That's fair," Tanaka said.

"Not if you're just going to stick them up your nose," Two-Can said.

"I'll eat them." Tanaka eyed the candy. They were even dirtier now, the orange coating grubby grey around the edge. Given a choice, he always went for candy straws. But he was hungry. He was always hungry.

"Save one for Ketchup," Two-Can reminded them.

"One? No way, José. We divide them evenly."

Tanaka leaned back against the wall and stuck his legs straight out, wondering whether somebody might trip over them, bash into the cigarette machine, and land in the ladies' washroom. Crash right through the door among the ladies on the toilet, with everybody screaming.

"Yeah." Flash held out his cupped hands and rubbed them together. Several candies fell to the ground again, and Two-Can picked them up. "If it had to be all one flavour, couldn't it be cherry?"

"Or grape," Tanaka agreed.

Even if they were cheap old orange, they were candy, and something about them felt more important than that. It took a real man to eat candy this dirty.

"Okay, start out with three candies."

They each took three in their palms and raised them to their mouths.

"Chug-a-lug," Flash said. "One, two …"

Two-Can said, "No, let's have glory or nothing. We'll double dare each other to do stuff. The one who wins gets …"

"All of 'em."

"Yeah. And the one who wins will be …"

"Rich? Handsome?" Tanaka said.

Flash held out both arms flat, like an ump's. "I know. The one who wins, we'll all have to watch him."

"Watch him eat them?"

"All. And wish we won. That'll be losing."

"Not bad," Two-Can admitted. He put his three in his pocket, but Flash wrestled for them and won. Flash was smaller than Two-Can, but he usually won. "Tanaka, you keep them. Your pocket has a zipper."

"First, double dare: you gotta get somebody to yell at you."

"May the best beazle win." Tanaka angled his foot behind Flash and Two-Can. He attempted to lever the cigarette machine over on its face, but it only squeaked forward slightly and banged back against the wall so that people in the seats looked at them but didn't yell.

Maybe kick the thing a little harder. Tanaka patted his back zip pocket, where the candies on their waxed paper crackled against his bum. He felt lucky.

Chapter 31

Jenny, don't come find me.

"Most people get a lot of chances." Jenny looked down at Adrian. He lay on the deck of the ship, not yet dried off, wrapped in a Hudson's Bay blanket courtesy of the ship's purser. Malcolm knelt at Adrian's side.

"I made it, didn't I?" Adrian looked up at Jenny. "Do me a favour, though. Don't let people know about me."

Malcolm said, "Everybody knows about you, Adrian."

"They don't."

"They do. Ask Jenny. She knows, and I didn't say a word about you and your goddamn sunshine-orange LSD."

"I hate you," Adrian murmured.

"I hate you more," Malcolm said. "You should have been badly injured, and you're not."

Jenny nodded at Malcolm. "This is how it should be."

"How what should be?" Malcolm asked.

She gestured to Adrian. "Friends should stick together, good times or bad."

"You're mixing us up with the Mouseketeers." Adrian flapped a hand and let it drop onto his chest. Jenny backed away. Her hair lifted in the hot wind from the engine room. Malcolm and Adrian were real. They mattered, and they were friends of hers. She looked from one to the other and decided, with the cold perspective that regret brings, that friendship was big enough to contain violence, and that love could be as smeared as candy on a child's face.

Don't come find me. The words played in her head like a pop song chorus. At a touch to her arm, she started.

Malcolm took his hand back and looked around as if wondering where to put it. He said, "I'm sorry about what happened out there on the deck. I thought you were in danger, and I wasn't sure whether I'd made an error in ingestion. I don't make a habit of taking drugs. I'm not that kind of person."

"I know." Jenny had no idea what he was talking about but sensed his relief at her reply. She studied his face and tried to remember what it felt like to kiss him.

"Won't you stay, Jenny? Help me get him upstairs." Malcolm indicated Adrian rolled in the striped blanket.

Don't come find me.

"I can't."

"Okay, then," he said. "Incidentally, I saw your cousin Frances on the car deck. You should go and find her."

"Sure." But she wouldn't. She felt cold all over. Hands, face and feet, chilly and numb. She put her hands into her pockets to warm them. In the bottom of her right pocket lay her Swiss Army knife.

Jenny, don't come find me. Joey's voice, imagined or real, led her upstairs to the passenger lounge. Here passengers snapped their newspapers from page to page or chattered with their elbows on the arms of their plastic bucket seats. Three kids in camper T-shirts tussled among themselves over by the cigarette machine. She narrowly missed tripping over one of them, but carried on and followed Joey's voice towards the women's washroom. She stepped inside into two inches of water, barely contained by the metal lip at the door. She guessed one of the sinks was plugged with the tap on so that it overflowed onto the floor. But she had to abandon logic and plumbing theories when the water rose swiftly past the lip of the closed door. This was no leak, but a flood. In a matter of seconds, the water covered her to her knees, her shoulders, and her head. A current picked her up and turned her around. She lost a flip-flop, and something revolved in front of her, shining in the water. Her knife. She reached for it, but the current pulled her sideways and she let it go.

Don't come find me. She should have known Joey was lying. She should have known he still wanted her.

She inhaled water, and it moved inside her lightly, like air. She took this for proof that she had passed back into the ghost world. Her second flip-flop floated away and she followed it, kicking up to the surface. She trod water and gazed about her at the Sound. The ferryboat was only a distant dash of white, but not far from her lay the water's edge and the jagged coastline thick with trees, mossy cliffs, and a rough brown beach. She swam towards shore, employing a sidestroke that sustained her strength. She swam until she cut her knee on a rock in the shallows and pulled herself onto the beach.

She called out, "Joey, come find me." When he didn't answer, she got to her feet and walked towards the cliff. It was as good a spot as any to begin searching.

Chapter 32

Frances stopped at the top of the stairs to the Sunshine Deck and brought a little logic to her search for Jenny. The downside of her career was her professional tendency to see complications in every endeavour. For example, she couldn't just shovel up a Roman mosaic; she had to wangle permissions, write out proposals, put a team together, and backstab at least one rival to the claim. But now that she was searching for Jenny on a large boat with multiple decks, she couldn't think like an archaeologist. She had to think like a damn mother.

She'd looked all over, even stumbling with false apologies into the captain's bridge, but now she saw she'd forgotten the simplest reason for a woman's disappearance. It beggared belief that she hadn't checked under the washroom cubicle doors for Jenny's feet in their flip-flops.

Frances smacked the rail with the flat of her hand and clattered upstairs to the passenger lounge. In her rush to the washroom door, she almost tripped over Tanaka, Two-Can, and Flash, who were leaning against the cigarette machine with their legs straight out in front of them.

"Watch it, Frances." Flash saluted her with a palm smeared with some kind of orange dye. And spit, probably. Tanaka caught at her leg with both hands, and she pulled loose, managing not to kick the boy.

Tanaka left a swirl of orange down her right leg and she stooped to rub at it, her eye on the washroom door.

She said, "Malcolm and Adrian are on board. Please transfer all debts and allegiances to them." The boys' grubby legs and stained hands beggared belief. "How did you get this dirty on a white boat?"

"We were dirty already," Flash explained. "We just moved it around."

"You were clean when I brought you on board." Frances snorted. "Did Jenny pass through here?"

Tanaka nodded, but Flash shrugged and Two-Can said, "Nah. Never seen her in our life."

They'd shown better manners in her charge, as well.

"What a long nose you have, Two-Can," Frances said.

Flash snickered. "Big nose, bigger boogers."

Somebody loved these kids, and Frances was glad it wasn't her. She stepped past them, giving the orange spot on her leg another rub. She put her hand on the door and left a smudge of orange under the sign that said 'Women'. The door was heavily sprung, and she had to lean on it to push through into the washroom. Something moved against her foot as she entered: a Swiss Army knife that spun away from her across the washroom floor. She picked it up and set it on the edge of one of the sinks in case its owner came looking for it.

The washroom was plastered in white stucco and busy with pipes. It contained three empty cubicles with their doors ajar, two sinks, and a roll of towelling on the wall. Jenny was nowhere to be seen.

Frances was no one's mother, and she wasn't worrying. If Jenny wasn't here, she was elsewhere. Frances would find her. She had a PhD, for God's sake.

She would find her, but first she would wash the orange smear off her leg.

Frances moved the knife up on top of the towel dispenser and turned on the tap—of course they were the sort of taps that, when you turned them on, turned back off, as if they were arguing with you and winning. You had to hold the cold tap on—the hot tap didn't work at all—and wash your hand by taking some phlegm-like soap from the container, contorting your hand under the stream of cold water and rubbing the thumb and four fingers together.

"What about one-handed people?" she asked the empty washroom. She scrubbed at her leg while the water pipes chuddered. "Nobody ever thinks about them."

A woman Frances couldn't see whispered several words, the meaning of which she couldn't make out over the ferry engine's hum and the noisy washroom plumbing. She gave herself a severe look in the small mirror over the sink and dried her hands on the roll of towelling. She turned to leave and heard the whisper again.

Come find me. Jenny's voice, faint and clear.

Frances peered around the first and second cubicle doors just in case, like Plato's cave, they were bigger inside than out.

Again she heard, *Come find me.*

Under the third half-open stall door she saw a flip-flop. It receded slowly, as if the girl had pulled herself farther up against the toilet. How could she have missed it? She was an overeducated fool. Jenny was here after all.

Frances pushed against the door. It opened slightly but caught on something, so that she had to bump it another inch or so inwards. She turned herself sideways and shoved.

Because the door was jammed, Frances had to pass through with the side of her face pressed against it. Her shoulder passed through, then her chest and the rest of her. She grabbed at the door catch, lost her grip and her balance, and slid sideways into deep water. She had no time to call for Jenny, only a couple of flailing seconds when she strove to keep her head above water and gasped a last breath. But it was clear the pull of the water was stronger than she was.

The water closed over her head.

Frances scissored her legs. She cast about for Jenny. White bubbles closed in, churned up, and blinded her.

Chapter 33

Malcolm found it hard going helping Adrian across the car deck towards the stairs.

The ferryboat topped another roller.

Adrian looped his arm over Malcolm's shoulder. "I feel like

the hero in some crappy World War II movie, and you're the private dragging me out of the firing lines."

"Why can't you be the private for once?"

"You have to be the private because you love to complain."

At the top of the steps, Malcolm looked around for Jenny. Was she avoiding him? He should never have kissed her. *You jump the gun and you pay, brother.*

He opened the lounge door and didn't see Jenny anywhere. Adrian pulled free of Malcolm's support, took two steps, and hung on to a chair. He nodded wearily across the lounge towards the cigarette machine. "There are our campers, damn their bright eyes."

Over by the women's washroom, Tanaka, Two-Can, and Flash sat cross-legged against the cigarette machine like the three wise monkeys they were not. Tanaka had his hands flat over his pockets, a sure sign he had something in there he shouldn't.

"What have you got in your pockets, Tanaka?" Malcolm asked.

"Fingernails," Tanaka replied.

"What else?"

"Dirt under my fingernails."

The door to the deck opened, and a woman juggling a toddler, a pack of cigarettes, and a Bic lighter entered, sat down, and lit up.

Adrian said, "I have a more important question. What are you kids doing on this boat? I told you to stay at camp."

Two-Can blew a raspberry. Flash folded his arms. The three boys wore the hard eyes you'd see on movie convicts.

"Come on, Two-Can," Malcolm said. "Don't act like that to a leader."

"I hate leaders and I hate camp." Flash turned and punched the machine behind him. He blew on his knuckles. "This stupid cigarette machine is more fun than camp."

Two-Can said, "We don't do anything at camp. It sucks rocks."

Tanaka said, "You leaders should teach us something. Teach us how to tie a knot."

Malcolm knew how to tie a sheepshank knot, and he said so.

Adrian shook his head. "Knots are for Boy Scouts. I'll teach you boys how to be cool. I'll teach you how to hide what you're thinking so that nobody knows anything about you."

Flash said, "That's not cool, that's stupid. Teach us how to gut a fish."

The woman smoking nearby said, "Don't you dare. Teach them not to kill living things. Teach them the *Moosewood Bible.*"

Her toddler squirmed down from her lap, his eyes on the three bigger boys. She held onto his collar.

Adrian sighed. "How old are you, lady? Thirty? At what point did you stop knowing how to be cool?"

"Well, junior, you don't stop knowing about cool, you stop caring. Only then will you really evolve into cooldom." She let go her toddler while she tapped her cigarette ash into the ashtray. "Also, I'm only twenty-six."

Malcolm couldn't see Jenny anywhere. He said, "You kids should listen to Adrian. Not showing your feelings could help you succeed in high school."

Adrian said, "And you'd win at poker. When you grow up, you could win a fortune at the gambling table."

"I would buy a million candies with it." Tanaka slipped his hand into his pocket. "How do we do cool, Adrian?"

Adrian looked at Malcolm. Malcolm shrugged.

"Shit," Adrian said, and he waved the word away as if it were an accidental fart. "Sit cross-legged, you three."

For only six legs, they made a big fuss about it . The toddler clambered over the back of the line of moulded seats and sat down on Tanaka's left in an apparent attempt to copy the boys, themselves intent on copying Adrian. Little fish copy bigger fish, Malcolm thought. It was all a circle game.

Adrian rested his butt on the back edge of a plastic seat. "Hands on your knees, index fingertip to thumb. Breathe in."

"We're breathing in that lady's smoke." Tanaka coughed expressively. The woman took a drag and beckoned to her tot, who paid her no heed.

"Ignore her. Now, breathe in … oh, I don't know. Breathe in all the lies of the world."

They breathed in with hideous playful sucking noises, but they held the lotus.

"Now breathe out the world's lies again."

Malcolm told himself he could leave the kids to Adrian. If only they weren't such idiots. "Stop breathing out so hard, Two-Can. You're going to kill yourself."

"Be *cool*."

In spite of himself, Malcolm evaluated the angle of Adrian's head and his loose shoulders and tried on his cool look.

Flash stood up. "Okay, I'm cool enough. Come on, guys." Tanaka followed, one fist clenched around something. The smoking woman's toddler scrambled to his feet beside them.

"Don't hog all the wax paper candy, Flash," Two-Can said. "Shit."

What wax paper candy?

Adrian looked over his shoulder at Malcolm. "Watch this. Two-Can Sam, don't say *shit*, say *crap*. And let's see that candy."

There was an odd look in Adrian's eye that Malcolm hadn't seen before. It might have been worry, and it might have been guilt.

"Don't even say *crap*," the woman with the cigarette snapped. "Paulie, come over here."

Paulie put out his lip at his mother.

Malcolm said, "You're a terrible teacher, Adrian."

"Shut up," Adrian said. "Shut your flapping mouth." He had never sounded more casual, but he rested a shaking hand on the cigarette machine. He said to Tanaka, "Give me the candy."

Tanaka put both hands behind him.

"What have you got?" Malcolm asked. He met Adrian's eyes and saw realization there. His head swam.

Adrian reached for the kid. "Tanaka, hand them over."

Malcolm took a step towards Flash, who was moving sideways towards the door.

"Just a second." Tanaka grinned, brought his hand out from behind him and raised it to his mouth.

Adrian batted at Tanaka's hand, and the orange *candies* on their sheets of wax paper winged across the floor around the three kids and the toddler. "Get the candies, Malcolm."

But Malcolm dived for the toddler. He pulled the child's fists from his mouth, wondering at the strength in a kid so small. He pried the little fingers open and retrieved three orange discs on wax paper, while the toddler screamed and his mother leapt to her feet. She stubbed out her smoke, snatched up her child and carried him out onto the deck. She would have sent them all to hell if she knew what had just happened. Almost happened.

Malcolm knelt in front of Tanaka, Flash, and Two-Can. "Did you eat any?"

"No." Tanaka looked up at him with round brown eyes, and Malcolm turned the kid around and unzipped the back pocket of his shorts, while Adrian pulled the pockets of the other two inside out.

Malcolm found himself standing in a public area holding a handful of orange Sunshine. LSD. He thrust the pills into his pocket. What was he supposed to do with them? Obviously the garbage can was not safe, and even flushing them down the toilet seemed less than responsible. He pictured an orange stream poisoning the ocean, spreading around the world, changing it forever. He ducked into the men's room and flushed the LSD anyway.

As he re-emerged, he heard a woman cry out.

Was that Jenny? He called her name. She didn't answer, and he called again.

He heard it clearly this time. *Come find me.*

Malcolm put his hand on the women's washroom door handle. It was the women's washroom, so he hesitated for a second. But then, he was new to this hero's life.

CHAPTER 34

Frances kicked off her shoes and let the air in her lungs raise her to the surface of the water. She didn't know how she had come to leave the ferryboat, but she wouldn't think about that now. She worked on getting her bearings among the waves. Thankfully these were not so big as to be unnegotiable, and she made out green-and-brown land a hundred yards or so away. She swam towards shore. Frances was a strong swimmer — she'd spent her childhood summers leaping off the pilings in Snug Cove with the big boys and sometimes even adults in semi-formal attire. Her arms and legs cut the water efficiently while her mind buzzed with the strangeness of passing through an interior door and finding herself in deep water. Frances rarely remembered her dreams, but she thought she'd remember this one.

It shouldn't matter in a dream whether she sank or swam, but the water was so cold and felt so real that it brought to mind the old wives' tale — that if you died in your dream, your heart failed and you died in your bed. But she didn't believe that, any more than she believed you could die of sorrow. The heart was a mighty engine which carried on for decades without maintenance or support. Still, Frances swam as if her life depended on it, and at length she skinned her knees in the shallows. She pulled herself up onto land and crawled onto a sunny outcrop of rock hanging over the water. The rock was padded with moss, and she lay on her back and looked up and around her. No sense in asking where she was, because nowhere in the world but in Howe Sound did sea and sky shine with this peculiar damp and pearly lustre. The mossy, deep-creviced rocks and the well-like shadows under the evergreens gave the air a rich taste, as if prepared from an ancient recipe to give long life and vigorous days.

Something pricked at her palms. She raised them to see her skin studded with tiny black periwinkles, which she brushed gently from her hands over the edge of the rock into the shallows.

Frances sat up. To her left, the mossy rocks; to her right there was a wide crevice, inside which a white curve gleamed against the shadows. She leaned closer and counted four fingers and a thumb reaching up. There was a statue in there. A statue she'd seen before, or one very like it.

She recognized these fingers, as graceful as a dancer's. She'd dug up a statue like this one long ago, outside Thessalonica. Of course, it had only been part of a statue, the hand and much of the arm. *Venus Bathing.* Although, Gig Chalmers said it was bound to be *Venus Rising.* She'd never found the rest of it, and so she'd never proven her thesis.

She got to her knees, reached deeper into the crevice, and touched the marble fingertips. Her own hands were so cold that the statue's fingers felt warm.

Out of the corner of her eye she saw a movement on the water, but she ignored it and reached further down between the rocks. She scraped her knuckles but found the slim wrist of the statue.

Above her head a raven squawked, and she looked up almost guiltily as it rattled through the trees before settling on a branch that dipped and rocked under its weight. A movement on the water caught her eye again. Somebody was moving across the water. Walking—no, dancing rather—and stopping now and then to look up at the blue sky.

A young woman, with long brown hair that the wind caught and lifted, was moving this way. Frances watched Jenny move towards her across the surface of the water.

She called out, and Jenny turned. Her double take was almost comical, but Frances didn't laugh. Jenny neared shore, shaking her stubborn young head.

"Frances, have you seen Joey?" Jenny stepped up to the rocks beside her. "I've been calling out for him to come find me for quite a long time."

"Joey's dead," Frances said. "Listen, there's something up here you should see."

"But he's here somewhere. I've waited, and I've looked. I don't understand why he hasn't come to me."

Frances said, "How can you understand dead people? They'll have totally different priorities. Take a look at what I've found in this crevice."

"He needs me."

"Needs you for what? Dead people don't need anything." Frances reached deeper, talking over her shoulder. "You can't bind their wounds or lend them money. You can't feed them or make love to them. Let well enough alone, Jenny."

Jenny said, "I lost him. I gave him up, and I want him back."

Frances held on tight to the statue's wrist. "It's hard work to stop hoping."

Jenny looked up sharply. "Where we are, this isn't suicide."

"Who said anything about suicide?" Frances stroked the statue's arm. The statue was hers, and Gig Chalmers would never get his eyes or hands on her.

Jenny said, "I'm here because that's how much I love him. He'll come find me, and then we'll be together."

"Sounds a pointless existence. What's life without work?" But Frances remembered what it was like to be twenty years old and wear gardenias on her wrist, loving a young man who didn't mind she wasn't too pretty if she made him laugh. She no longer remembered his name. She said, "*Men have died, and worms have eaten them, but not for love.*"

"That's a lie," Jenny said.

"Yes, yes, Shakespeare lied. And there are no such things as walking dead men, Jenny Riley. Come here and look at this. The shadows of the trees above cooled Frances's neck as she held fast to the white marble hand.

With a rattle of pebbles, Jenny climbed up on the rock beside her.

"No hurry." Frances pulled on the hand, and it shifted a little. So it might very well be only a hand and forearm like the one she'd found long ago. Not a complete statue. She would have to take care not to scratch it, sliding it out and up. She had no tools, but the moss here on the rock would cushion the marble as she retrieved it. If the rest of Venus was down there, she would be in pieces. Still, Frances could reassemble her. She would love above all things to reassemble her. She wished she had tools with her, even the Swiss Army knife she'd left in the women's washroom. She looked up to see Jenny at her side, looking down.

Frances stroked the statue's fingers and did her best to explain. "It's *Venus Bathing*. Only a fool would think it was *Venus Rising*. Or—and I never told Gig Chalmers this—what I'm looking for, what I'd kill to find, is *Venus with Cupid*, her child."

Jenny touched Frances's arm. Frances was pleased that her young cousin cared, but honestly she needed some help. "I'm going to haul her out piece by piece. I think I can get the hand out intact. Missed that coup in '58, but I got my doctorate out of the bits."

"This is the ghost world, Frances," Jenny said. "I followed Joey because I love him. You followed me in. Does that mean you love me, Frances?"

"We're blood relations. Of course I do." The girl would never make an academic at this rate. "I'm not the only one."

Frances felt Jenny's start of surprise. Jenny asked, "Who else loves me?"

"Who do you think?"

"Joey."

Frances looked longingly down at the marble hand. This sort of work was the best work in the world, and it took patience. Frances had patience. She showed her patience now. She didn't say Joey never loved Jenny, although it was an obvious conclusion. She slid sideways on her conviction and said only, "Joey's on a different list. It's your friends and family who love you."

Jenny frowned. "I can't remember who that would be."

"You will, difficult girl. And don't forget the boys who admire you on the street."

"Frances, that's not love."

"It's a kind of love, an archetype of love," Frances told her.

"Who else?"

"Rachel loves you."

Frances became aware of Jenny's silence. She looked up from the statue to see that Jenny had moved away from her on the rock.

"Rachel *would* follow me," Jenny said. "Rachel always follows me."

"And that Chinese boy, Malcolm," Frances said. "He'd follow you."

Jenny made a choking sound. "You're right. Malcolm, too. Like you. They'll all leave the real world. They'll all end up here in the ghost world. They'll end up dead like you and me. And Joey."

"Listen, I've got to get down to work." Frances had patience and a passion to know. Work was her true love. Work was her child. She looked into the crevice again and drew in her breath. How had she thought the hand was a statue's? The fingers were too thin, and now she saw that they were bones. Bones to extract from the crevice.

Even better, in a way. What a find.

Jenny stood up. "What if I broke something somewhere? What if all of you heard me call, and you all left their lives and came here?"

Frances heard Jenny take a deep preparatory breath, the sort of breath you take before you scream.

She wouldn't.

She did. Jenny screamed like a seabird, and then like the siren on a ferryboat. The sound was a nail through Frances's head. She closed her eyes and blacked out while Jenny's cry took over the world.

Chapter 35

Malcolm burst through the washroom door and found Jenny sitting on the floor with her back against the wall under the towel dispenser. Frances lay beside her, her lower half under a cubicle door, her head in Jenny's lap.

Malcolm crouched down on the floor beside them.

"Is she sick?" Malcolm asked Jenny. "Is it her heart?"

"I don't know."

"Shall I carry her out of here? Or should I carry you?" Malcolm shifted from one foot to the other. It wasn't that Frances looked very heavy, but the angles of a human body would be awkward to manage.

"Frances is waking up," Jenny said.

"No, she isn't," Frances said, eyes closed. "She doesn't want to. She wants what she found in the rock crevice by the sea."

"Malcolm, can you bring me a wet cloth?"

Malcolm looked around and got his shirt halfway off before he thought of the towel dispenser across the room. He hauled on the cotton towelling until he felt the mechanism inside break and it bloused out onto the floor. He pulled harder and a yard of cotton rolled out, still attached at both ends but long enough to reach the sink. He soaked a length of it and pulled it farther out until the white fabric spanned the washroom.

"It's like a Möbius strip." Malcolm patted at Frances's temples while Jenny wet her wrists. "It goes on forever and never stops."

"That's a redundant statement," Frances murmured.

"I always wanted to know how much towelling was in one of these dispensers," Malcolm said. Jenny laughed unsteadily. She looked into his eyes at last, and he decided that it was the laugh that had done it. He made a mental note to keep making her laugh.

A patch of red on the floor under one of the sinks caught his eye. A Swiss Army Knife. He stretched full out to retrieve it.

Frances sat up, got to her knees, and hauled herself up to the sink. There was a sudden bump that swayed the doors to the cubicles. She said, "The boat's docking."

Jenny frowned. "Which landing? Island or mainland?"

"Mainland," Frances said.

"The island," Malcolm said at the same moment. "Sorry. I don't need to be right."

"What an attractive and unusual boy you are," Frances said tiredly. "I don't care if we're docking in Mexico. I want off this boat."

With an effort, Malcolm held the door open for her.

Jenny followed Frances, but Malcolm stopped her with a touch. They both looked at his hand against her bare arm, and he dropped it. He leaned his back on the washroom door to hold it open and said, "I'm sorry for the kiss. Is this your knife?"

"It is. Thanks. Thanks for coming to find me. I feel like I want to give you something. Do you want the knife?"

"I don't."

She inclined her head. "I don't know what, then." She held up her empty hands to him.

"Just what I wanted," Malcolm said. He took her hands in his and curled his fingers around her palms. She looked at their clasped hands and stood for a moment as still as a statue.

She said, "These worlds all look the same. Ghost world, real world. How do I tell which one we're in?"

Malcolm wanted to beg her not to be crazy, because if she was crazy it would be so much more difficult and time-consuming to win her affections.

Instead, he said lightly, "Hey, let me know if you figure it out."

Chapter 36

As a favour to Frances, who knew the captain, the ferryboat staff did not tow her green Galaxie off the ferryboat. Instead it sailed back and forth across the Sound for the rest of the afternoon, shining in the sunlight, and sat on the deck all through the night. Just before noon the next day, Frances found her spare keys on the bookshelf in her living room, between Kingsley's *Heroes* and *I'm Okay, You're Okay*. She walked the half-hour to the meet the ferry and retrieve her car. She stood on the dock, watching the ferry's slow approach, smelling herring from a fishing boat and coffee from a yacht, growing hungry and impatient. The ferry was always late in summer. You'd think they'd allow for the traffic, but no. It was the same every year, but that was the great thing about living on an island. Everything was always the same, and even if there was a change, pretty soon that was the same every year, too.

A battered pickup with *Camp Vehicle* stencilled on the door creaked to a stop near Frances. Jenny leapt down from the truck bed, banged her palm on the side panel, and it growled away.

"About time, too." Frances jingled her keys in her pocket.

"I wish you didn't have to leave for England," Jenny said.

Frances looked hard at her cousin but could see no sign of irony. "It won't be the same without you, difficult girl."

"They'll probably hire me on at the camp, anyway. I can cook."

Frances grimaced. "I have to go. England would miss me." She dug her fingernails into her palms inside her pockets. If she didn't go, it would be Gig Chalmers's name in brass on the wall of the British Museum. She attempted to picture the Hertfordshire mosaic as she'd seen it on her last visit in February: the varieties of shape and colour that would almost certainly be revealed as Orpheus with his lyre, leading pale Eurydice out of the world of the dead. But Frances couldn't picture it. Instead she remembered running down to this very spot on the Bowen Island dock every summer's evening when she was young. She would sit outside the dance hall among the laughing, shoving bigger girls in their trousers and heels, in their draped skirts and curly hairdos. Frances would hum along with the band through mouthfuls of lemon sherbet or Mrs Docharty's pies. With her back to the open windows, she'd sit and kick her heels among the skirts and trousers, light spilling over her and out into the darkness. Frances watched the band, slick-haired and white-jacketed, and saw how their shadowed eyes followed the prettiest girls around the room. The dance floor shone red under the dancers' feet—red wood, with a bit of a bounce, as Frances knew from loosening the shutters one grey morning in her childhood and dancing in the middle of the red floor all by herself. It had moved a little underneath her tennis shoes. It had almost danced back. When the municipality tore down the dance hall, they sold the red boards to some of the islanders. They formed Frances's living room floor, for example, and she sometimes felt them move under her feet for no reason, except maybe remembrance. Decades later, here on the dock with her hair greying and a different boat coming in, Frances missed those black-and-yellow nights. She felt sorry for Jenny, who didn't even have that memory.

Frances shaded her eyes and scanned the boat deck. "There's the Galaxie."

"There's a girl sitting on the hood." Jenny leaned out, and Frances pulled her back.

Frances handed her keys to Jenny. "Drive the Galaxie off the boat and park at the general store."

"What do I do with the girl?" Jenny asked, but ran to the head of the line-up before Frances could answer.

When the cars were unloaded, the ferry workers waved Jenny on board. Frances watched the two girls climb inside the car, Jenny taking the wheel. The Galaxie clunked up the ramp, and Frances followed it up the hill to the general store. She pulled open the passenger door and the girl climbed out.

"Did I invite you?" Frances asked Rachel. "I can't recall."

"Jenny called me. She said, 'Come find me.'" Jenny's sister hugged a backpack to her chest and looked up at Frances. "So I came."

"Where's your independent spirit? Do you always have to do everything Jenny says?"

"Kind of."

"Why are you here?" The girl was too pale for summer. Had

she been sitting in her room all through the fine weather? What would cause a young girl to do that?

"I'm striving to be happy." Rachel bit her lip. "But the thing is, I have the weirdest feeling that anybody who's not here right now doesn't actually exist. Have you ever thought about that? Have you ever thought that only what you see exists? That there's nothing over that hill, and nothing behind the general store, until we walk back there? If I went back there, they'd have to build it and tear it down when I left."

"Wasn't there a *Twilight Zone* episode about that?" Frances asked. "But don't listen to me: test out your theory."

"How?"

"Run behind the general store as fast as you can, and see if you can surprise somebody building the back parking lot and creating the beaches and hillsides on the far side."

Rachel ran off behind the store. A moment later she returned.

"What happened? Was the back parking lot there?" Frances lifted one eyebrow. Rachel was an easier case than Jenny.

Rachel nodded. "But you and Jenny weren't. Where did you go when I was out of your sight? Did you disappear? Were you anywhere? Was it all black nothingness when I was gone?"

"Oh lord. Does it ever stop?" Frances sucked her upper lip. "I should tell you about the pragmatists, who believed nothing exists but what you can see. And I'd better tell you about the sceptics as well, for balance."

"I'd like to be a sceptic," Jenny said. "I'd like to stop believing in certain things."

"You know where I keep my books. Knock yourself out. Incidentally, Rachel, you'll have to share a room with Jenny until I leave for England."

Frances had no idea how she was going to leave these two alone together, but archaeology had to come before crazy young cousins who washed up on her island. She would not get used to having Jenny and Rachel at her side. And, more, she would not feel her heart lift in a motherly fashion as those two young men came striding up to the general store parking lot. Dark and blond, Malcolm and (God help her) Adrian.

And, even worse: down the hill ran three little boys, whooping right towards her.

Tanaka, Two-Can, and Flash. No question, they were going to knock her over. And their hands would be as sticky as used jelly donuts.

They ran to her and wrapped their grubby arms around her middle.

A person could get used to not being alone. *Damn.* She hated the thought of giving up that dig to Chalmers. But she'd have foreign soil on her hands again someday, and in the fullness of time she'd hold ancient treasures up to the light. Or, more likely, ancient rubbish. Although at this distance, treasure and rubbish were the same.

Well, here it was: she decided to give her dig in Hertfordshire to Gig Chalmers, damn his eyes. And for a reward, she was rooted into this tree-and-water island, entirely surrounded by a ragtag band of what felt exactly like friends and family.

After a lifetime of leaving everybody, wanting nobody, Frances couldn't leave these young ones. They didn't have to say they needed her—she'd bet you couldn't even pay them to—but they did. She smiled over the heads of the little boys at the two young women she was going to host all summer long. She felt pleased and, if she was honest with herself, a little sorry for Gig Chalmers.

Anyway, you had to have somebody who'd care if you died.

Chapter 37

"It's eleven o'clock in the morning. Get up," Malcolm said. He picked a broken flip-flop off the floor and threw it through a spider web in the corner of the cabin.

"I can't get up. Not until lunch. I'm in love." Adrian sat up, apparently naked in his sleeping bag. He coughed and spat out the cabin window. He sounded like crap, but in the semi-gloom he looked the picture of handsome health.

"You're not in love."

"Then maybe I can't get up because you're in love." Adrian hung a bare leg over the bunk rail.

Malcolm said, "Take the kids down to look for crabs on the beach or something. Earn your pay cheque."

"Nah. I'd rather get paid to lie here talking about romance." Adrian turned on his side and rested his head on his fist. "The thing that everyone does wrong in love, Malcolm, is to sit back and let it happen."

"Baloney." Malcolm pictured Jenny loping down the hill ahead of him, her hair swinging the way it did, most of the way down her back to her waist. He saw in his mind's eye the lift of her heels, almost a skip, which propelled her up as well as forward. He'd never seen a girl move exactly like that, and he was as certain as he could be that he was the first person who had ever noticed the unique way she walked. God, she was lovely.

Malcolm put both hands to his forehead. "I always thought a girl would just, you know, come along."

Adrian said, "That's your mother talking, and your mother is full of shit. I guess she's right about a few things, though."

"What my mother actually said was, the right girl would come along and walk by me like I was invisible."

"The thing is not to get your love advice from anybody born earlier than 1952."

"You're right." Malcolm slung a filthy, wet sock into the bottom bunk. "My mother, to my certain knowledge, went to dances and danced with anybody who asked her."

"The slut. What does that have to do with love in the time of NBC?" Adrian rolled so that his chin rested on the side of the bunk. He looked almost alert. "*Love American Style.*"

"What?"

"*Love American Style.* Stupid show, but you learn that there's somebody for everybody."

"Oh, for God's sake. Get out of bed."

"No. Literature next. Examples, please." Adrian made the buzzer noise from *Reach for the Top.*

"I don't know. *Love Story?*"

"You call that literature? Fine. The lesson is to love them quick before they die. *Nixon.*"

"Nixon? The president's not a TV show."

"Nixon on the news is proof that nothing will ever change. That's important information for young people in love."

"Everything changes."

"Hardly anything." Adrian hung one leg out through the zipper of his bag.

"Science changes. Music changes."

"It has to, or they'd play the same five songs every hour until we died."

"*10cc* is new," Malcolm insisted. "*I'm Not in Love.* Outstanding."

Adrian countered with, "Andy Kim. 'Rock Me Gently'."

"Andy Kim of the *Archies?*"

"You don't get him. Andy Kim, man. The guy's got great range."

Malcolm nodded. "How do you do it? I mean, you're an idiot and you do everything wrong, but it still turns out right."

Adrian shrugged. "Will you stop goddamn admiring me? I've been taking this shit from you for too long. I've had enough. Let me *be* a bastard, and you go on being the lord of all that is intelligent, heroic, and worthy."

"I don't admire you," Malcolm protested, remembering even so the great arc that Adrian had carved in the air when he sprang from the ship's rail. It was the most irrational thing he'd ever see anybody do, but Adrian shone like an angel all the way down to the water. "I don't even like you very much."

"You idiot," Adrian said. "You don't get my compliment."

"I don't want your compliment," Malcolm lied. He could still feel the cotton of Jenny's shirt in the centre of his palm from when he kissed her in the hospital foyer. He remembered how her long hair slipped between his thumb and index finger when he pushed a strand away from her cheek.

He cleared his throat and searched for something to say. "Still want to be a teacher?" Malcolm asked Adrian.

"Yeah. I think I'd be good."

Malcolm laughed. He held out his hand.

Adrian swore. He reached under his pillow, and into Malcolm's palm he placed an orange pill.

"Any more in your pants pockets?"

Adrian reached into the pocket of the shorts hanging on the bunk rail. "Nope, not even change."

"Too bad," Malcolm told him. "Change is good."

Adrian flung his pillow, sleeping bag, and a pair of Y-front gonch onto the floor. He sat up again, clad after all in cut-offs. "Oh, go ahead and try for Jenny. Just keep your cool."

"I'm always cool." Malcolm headed for the door.

"You're always *around*. Malcolm?"

"Yeah." He'd keep looking until he found her, or a telephone at least to call her up.

"When you talk to Jenny, don't forget to say something unique."

"Say what, exactly?" Malcolm stopped dead at the doorway and looked back. One minute ago he knew what he had to do, and now certainty was squeezing out between his fingers. "I was thinking of making her laugh."

"You know a joke? Okay, but don't just stammer stuff. Ask her a musical question."

A musical question. "I don't know any musical questions. Do they even have them anymore? They did in the thirties, they did in the forties. My mother, your mother ..."

"Malcolm."

"What?" He'd have to put on a clean shirt, although not if he phoned her.

Adrian threw the filthy sock at Malcolm's head. "Tell her a joke."

Chapter 38

Joey had never seen a darker night — not since he'd died, anyway.

"I'd never go anywhere with you." Moira was the kind of girl who knew how to challenge a man. Tease him. Her methods were basic but effective. "Not if you were the last guy on earth."

"And I am that last guy. You're stuck with me, sweetheart." Joey's arm slipped around her shoulder, and over their heads stars appeared in a silver cluster. "Isn't this a starlit moment?"

"Those aren't stars," she told him. "That's a mirror ball, from the dance hall."

He said, "Let's pretend it's the moon, and that's the sky."

"Let's pretend there's a swinging band and we're singing while we dance."

She hummed in his ear, a tickling, tuneless buzz.

Moira was right: the silver ball twinkled overhead. Beneath it a bandleader in a grimy-cuffed white dinner jacket crooned a song Joey knew, if he could only remember that crazy first line.

Moira leaned her head on his chest. She sang, "*Moonlight and roses . . .* Do you believe in love at first sight?"

Over her shoulder, as he held her, Joey made a face. "No."

But he remembered Jenny at six, the day she moved in next door. The feathers of her hair had waved against the curve of her cheek as she leaned out her window to offer him her soft hand. Even in childhood, she was all he ever wanted. After dying in a car crash was a hell of a time to find that out.

"I believe in love at first sight." Moira sighed, her breath warm against his chest as they danced. The mirror ball twinkled. "I think it's wonderful how the world brings two unlikely people together."

"You're a romantic?" The corner of Joey's mouth twisted. "Romantic girls are always the most interesting."

"Are you romantic too?" She looked up at him through her lashes. *Basic but effective.* Well, he knew a few moves, too.

"Watch this." Joey closed his eyes and drew her closer. He was impressed with the slender curve of her waist. He could have reached his arm right around two of her, and he liked that, as well as the feel of her young limbs when the music slowed, and the way she wound her arms around his neck like a string of Christmas lights.

He danced them off the floor and up, past the mirror ball into the darkness above.

He was a good dancer. Why didn't he ever know that about himself? He bet he would have played piano well, too, if he'd only tried. If he'd only had time. Well, you could only do so much in twenty-two years. James Dean had had more time than that.

"I was too busy with Jenny." He looked down at the spinning world shining below them like the mirror ball overhead.

"Don't talk about other girls." Moira swayed in his arms.

Joey wished Moira were blonde, white-haired, and heavy-lidded like Harlow.

"I was too busy saving Jenny from danger."

Moira laughed, a witch's cackle. Her hair smelled like seawater. He held her tight as they spiralled upwards.

He murmured, "God, I hate that Malcolm."

"Talking about people I don't know. You've got worse-than-average manners, haven't you, Joe?"

Joey didn't know whether he meant what he said next, but he said it anyway. He said it out loud. "I'm glad you've got more time than I had, Jenny."

He ought to get some credit for saying that.

The young woman in Joey's arms looked up into his eyes, and he felt a touch at his heart that opened something inside him. In spite of everything he believed he was, and everything the living world thought he should be, his heart warmed and beat hard against his chest. Which was good, because he was pretty sure he was stuck with this woman for a foreseeable eternity.

Moira said, "You're kind of sweet, my average Joe."

He answered like Bogart. "We're made for each other, baby."

She leaned her head against his shoulder, and he danced them higher into the night.

Chapter 39

Doctor, doctor, will I die?
Close your eyes and count to five.
One, two, three, four, five — I'm ...

... alive. In the land of the living. Yes or no? Several indications favoured it. Jenny squirmed against the moss that had found its way down the back of her bathing suit. The rocky ledge next to the red-railed Mount Gardner dock was no sandy Hawaiian beach. She shielded the sun from her eyes with one hand and scratched under her strap with the other.

At her side, Malcolm was telling her some kind of funny story in a fierce monotone. "So the man goes up to the desk to ask for a bus schedule. He says, 'Excuse me, *Miss Information*?'"

There was a pause, in which the sound of young campers bickering on the dock grew louder. Malcolm cleared his throat.

"That's your joke?" Jenny asked. "I'm just making sure."

"It's the only joke I can ever remember."

Above them the July sun shone so brightly it was almost as if the sky reflected the sea instead of the other way around. She was sharing her towel with Malcolm — apparently no male believed in bringing towels to water activities, for the little boys had brought nothing at all beyond the swim trunks that they had to hike up over bony pelvises every other minute. They hurled themselves off the dock, scrambled back up, and flung themselves down on the rough cedar planks to dry for a moment before they splashed back in again. They pushed and swore. Lying on her rock a little too close to their splashes, Jenny was glad she was not a little boy; she was pretty sure they wouldn't change places with her, either. Another spray of water splashed across her legs, and she pulled in her feet so her knees were sticking up. Cold water and a quick reaction time were further positive indicators that she was among the living.

She shaded her eyes and gazed over Malcolm's hairless, golden chest. Above his ribs, the nipples sat up straight. His stomach was flat and narrow.

She said, "I'm a little jealous about your stomach."

"Sorry." Malcolm craned his neck. "Is Ketchup still alive?"

Ketchup was not allowed in the water because of the cast on his arm. He'd brought an inner tube and was floating around the rest of the seal-headed little boys, hitting them with the rubber sides of his craft. His cast would have been soaked by now if Malcolm hadn't masking-taped a plastic bread bag around it.

Jenny shifted as the rock beneath them scratched at the area where her shoulder met the back of her arm. She breathed in the smell of cedar and lime rickey. Discarded paper cups, sticky and green, were piled on the moss beside Malcolm, next to the wax paper from a dozen sandwiches. She didn't think he'd seen the tiny black ants swarm the cups beside his elbow, but it was only a matter of time until he did and the cups went flying. She said, "The first time I met Joey was the day I moved in next door, and he found a plank somewhere. He slung it between our windows and told me to climb across."

"How far down?"

"Eighteen feet."

"That Joey, what a hero."

Malcolm's ribs rose and fell under his tight golden skin. He was a very beautiful young man.

Jenny frowned. She wished she could write down what she wanted to say so as to get it right. "I don't know if I want … It seems so terrible, to try really loving anybody. You, I mean. The intensity of everything, the responsibility, and when romance goes bad it's like a big portal leading into darkness …"

Malcolm stirred, raised himself on his elbow, and peered at her. "That doesn't sound like love. That sounds like graduate school."

She snorted. "Hey, a real joke."

Malcolm looked pleased—until she continued, "Anyway, I don't know any other way to love anybody." It was a foolish statement to make, and it hung there between them like a fug of smoke until she realized it was not only foolish but also untrue.

Malcolm lay back down at her side, shaking his head. "I think you just got in with the wrong person. Like me. When Adrian and I were six, he wanted to blow caps on the train tracks. I was supposed to lay the caps."

"Like I had to crawl across Joey's board bridge. But maybe we'd be cowards without them."

Malcolm screwed up his face. Jenny decided to give him a moment to recover from disagreeing with her. She gazed over at the dock, where Adrian lay sprawled out between Rachel and Frances. Frances sat with her legs crossed under her, reading aloud to them from *I'm Okay, You're Okay.*

A tree over the rocks thrashed wildly, as if in a high wind. Malcolm sat up. "Tanaka and Flash, get down out of that tree.

It's too young to take your weight."

Flash yelled, "We're young too, and we're never coming down."

Tanaka called, "It's the *Freakies* tree, you old Boss-moss."

Rachel clambered to her feet and set both hands on her hips. "*I'll* get them down."

Rachel was always around these days, lying on the dock and listening to every word she and Malcolm said. Jenny had a feeling her sister disapproved of all romance, but she wasn't sure, because Rachel seemed unable to take her eyes off Malcolm's golden torso.

"Get down," Rachel bellowed into the tree. She wore a swimsuit she'd pulled out of the attic back home in Vancouver. It was blue and had sleeves.

"Stupid girl," Ketchup shouted.

"Sexist pig," Rachel returned.

There came long, indrawn boyish breaths. "She said *sex*. Sexy! Sexy girl."

"*Boys are rotten,*" Rachel sang.

"*Made out of cotton,*" Jenny called.

"*Girls are sexy, made out of Pepsi.*"

Malcolm rolled his head to the side and met Jenny's eyes. "Am I supposed to talk about the next time I will kiss you? How communicative do you think we should be?"

Jenny smiled. "*Girls go to college to get more knowledge.*"

"*Boys go to Jupiter to get even stupider.*"

The tree branches where the little boys sat rained tiny brown cones onto Rachel's head.

"The next time you kiss me ..." Jenny folded her hands on her stomach. "Don't ask me, Malcolm. A kiss is supposed to be a surprise."

"Damn. I wish I were a girl," Malcolm told her.

"Interesting."

"I mean it. I wish I had it easy and could just lie there like you do right now, all creamy skin in your bathing suit and somebody wants to kiss you."

Jenny laced her fingers and looked through them at the lattice of blue and green light. "You know everything, but you don't know anything, Malcolm Lee."

But he must have learned something, because when she gave him her narrowest gaze, the one no one ever got past—except Joey—Malcolm leaned close and kissed her, a light kiss on the lips.

There was a scream of horror from the tree.

"Not in front of the children," Jenny told him. "And you should know that I have a rule that I only kiss at night."

"I see." Malcolm nodded. His black hair caught the sunlight. He kissed her again.

Jenny stood up and brushed moss out of her hair.

"Stay away from the water, you boys," Frances shouted from the dock. She put down the book. Beside her, Adrian appeared to be asleep. Frances tucked a car blanket over him as if he were a little child and not the great bruised creature of beauty that he was. "And Jenny, no kissing."

"Sure," Jenny lied. She remembered that she was trying not to lie and added, "Frances, I yam what I yam."

She climbed up onto the ramp and leaned against the red railing. She looked down and then out. Blue out to sea, brown looking down. The underside of the ramp was reflected in the water, a dark rectangle that looked like a door. If she jumped, she would pass right through the centre of it.

Jump off the dock. It was her own voice. Her inner voice. She was sure of that.

Look how dark the water is.

It's deep red, like blood.

The colour was a reflection of the red dock railings.

There are rocks down there. And who knows what else, waiting a fingertip away on the other side of the door.

Jenny climbed up on the rail. There was nothing to hold on to, and one foot slipped on the red-painted surface. She righted herself.

The more often you pass through into the ghost world, the easier it is. Do you even know which world you're in right now?

There were so many worlds, though—not just those of the living and the dead. Invisible worlds. Natural worlds that only existed away from the busy hands of people. All worlds shared so many elements that it was easy to become confused. For example, looking across to the mainland wilderness, she was seeing the world exactly as it would have looked thirty, a hundred, and a thousand years ago. Still, she was almost certain she and the others here by the dock were in the world of this time and this year, layered over the world of Moira's time before the steamships were scrapped and the car ferries ran. There were less obvious worlds within worlds, as well, like the childhood world into which no grownup could enter, and individual worlds of sorrow that no one else could penetrate or understand.

Across the Sound, sunlight made a path on the water where Moira had walked.

Everything died in the end, as Joey said. But first, everything sprouted and grew up green. Everything reached its full height and toppled. For example, these trees around Mount Gardner Bay. New growth rose out of fallen trees, red as frogs' bellies. Nothing really died. No one who lived in this green and growing forest beside that shining sea could ever die. The elements would not permit the waste of life. Everything lived, and went on living, with dogged beauty and deep roots.

Maybe world called to world, *Come and find me.*

She was still not certain which world she was in now.

Jenny took a deep breath, raised both arms above her head, pushed with her toes against the red dock rail, and arched into a dive.

She entered the water and opened her eyes. Her hair rose as she descended, and bubbles escaped her nose and mouth, brushing her forehead as they left her. She tasted salt in the back of her throat. It was a mess of light and dark down here, but she made out two distinct figures. A hand touched hers.

Jenny peered through a million, a billion, an infinity of bubbles, each one shiny as young life, and met Malcolm's gaze. His hands moved to circle her waist, and his skin was warm against her belly. They rose and broke the water.

Malcolm gasped and wiped at his nose. Beside them the second figure resolved into a large seal. It surfaced, watched the two of them for a moment, and sank back down again. Jenny felt the round cool hairiness of the seal's flank brush her leg as it swam away.

Somebody called her name, and Jenny bobbed around to look up at the gangway over the water.

The four little boys stood on the red rail, shifting from foot to foot like birds on a telephone wire.

Tanaka looked down at Jenny and Malcolm, slapped his own bum, and sang, *"Ass-k me no more questions, tell me no more lies …"*

Flash yelled, *"The boys are in the washroom, pulling up their …"*

Ketchup: *"… flies are in the city, the bees are in the park …"*

Two-Can: *"… and Jenny and Malcolm are kissing in the dark."*

"D-A-R-K." Faces turned up, eyes screwed shut, the boys in their bright bathing suits jumped off the red dock, and the

water blossomed around them. Rachel shrieked and jumped off the dock into the jumble. Jenny trod water in a circle at the centre of everything. She splashed a fan of water over Adrian, and he reached a languorous hand over the edge of the dock and splashed Malcolm, who swam over beside her. She could feel the touch of his fingertips as he swirled his arms around him, treading water. This moment was not significant on any international scale, but it was important to Jenny personally. She named it The Moment of Children and Adults at Play. She smiled to see them bob up and down on the surface of the water, while underneath, where she couldn't see, shiners and minnows skittered through the water like rays of sunlight through breaks in the clouds. Jenny splashed her sister, and Rachel made an outraged face and splashed her back with both hands. Then she turned belly up and power-kicked a fountain that rained down on everyone. Jenny named this The Moment of Rachel Splashing.

Now there was another small but vital turning, in which Frances leapt into the water fully clothed. Jenny decided that while Frances jumped, that moment was all there was, and now it was in her past and would never come again. But there would be a next moment, and a next, all in a line and never repeated, beyond intentional repetitions, like having the same thing for breakfast — strawberry flavoured milk, maybe, and cereal shaped like tiny monsters — and circular enjoyments like climbing out of the water, as she did now, running up the ramp, and swinging herself up to stand on the railing to feel the joy of slicing through the air and water, and to feel the cool of the darkness undersea. Shadows and light. Up and down. Yes and no. Alive. Yes.

Just yes.

Also by Mel Anastasiou

THE EXTRA: A MONUMENT STUDIOS MYSTERY

Vancouver schoolmarm Frankie Ray runs away to Silver Screen Hollywood to test her conviction that an actress who lacks glamour but has talent and an enterprising attitude can make it in the movies. But when a dissolute, womanizing matinee idol turns up dead on her sofa, Frankie's career hopes shatter. She'll need all her acting chops to sleuth out the murderer and clear her name.

STELLA RYMAN AND THE FAIRMOUNT MANOR MYSTERIES

On this particular sun-and-shade April morning at Fairmount Manor, Stella Ryman no more entertained the idea of becoming an amateur sleuth than she did of entering next spring's Boston Marathon. For not only was Stella eighty-two years old, but she had lately sold her home and a lifetime of gathered possessions and washed up at Fairmount Manor Care Home in such a state that she would have bet her remaining seven pairs of socks that she'd be dead in half a year.

THE LABOURS OF MRS STELLA RYMAN:
FURTHER FAIRMOUNT MANOR MYSTERIES

When the machineries of institution fail to protect Fairmount Manor, octogenarian amateur sleuth Mrs Stella Ryman rolls up her fleece jacket sleeves to protect Fairmount from a thief, investigate a gun-toting resident, set right a mishandled investigation of a man's death, pursue spectres and footpads walking at midnight, and discover Thelma Hu's long-lost fortune. No good deed goes unpunished, though, and Stella will face struggles, mysteries, and sacrifices that hit her where she lives.

PULPLITERATURE.COM

THE ARTISTS

Kristina Gehrmann

Cover artist, Erebus and Terror at Beechey Island

Kristina Gehrmann is an illustrator and graphic novelist who explores historical and fantasy subjects in a detailed painterly style. Her preferred tools are a Wacom tablet and Photoshop. Kristina's graphic novel debut, *Im Eisland,* tells the story of the lost Franklin Expedition in a trilogy of three books, the first of which won the German Children's Literature Award in 2016. She is deaf since birth, and currently lives in Hamburg, Germany, with her husband.

Erebus and Terror at Beechey Island is from a period in which Kristina experimented with watercolours and was exploring her fascination with the Franklin Expedition. In this painting, the ships Erebus and Terror are overwintering in the pack ice during their first winter (1845–46), when things were still going relatively well for the ultimately doomed expedition.

Artyom Trakhanov

Illustrator, 'A Cold Place Between the Shores'

Artyom Trakhanov is a notorious Slavic nihilist, dedicated to creating comics in two genres: folk horror and sci-fi eco-thrillers. His work appears in *Undertow,* Turncoat, *The 7 Deadly Sins, First Knife,* and elsewhere.

Mel Anastasiou
In-house illustrator

Mel Anastasiou loves drawing for *Pulp Literature* because she loves the stories she illustrates. She draws in black and white, working from imagination and inspired by details from Renaissance compositions. You can find illustrations, writing tips, and news about her books and novellas at melanastasiou.wordpress.com, and see more of her artwork on Facebook at Bird and Branch Artwork.

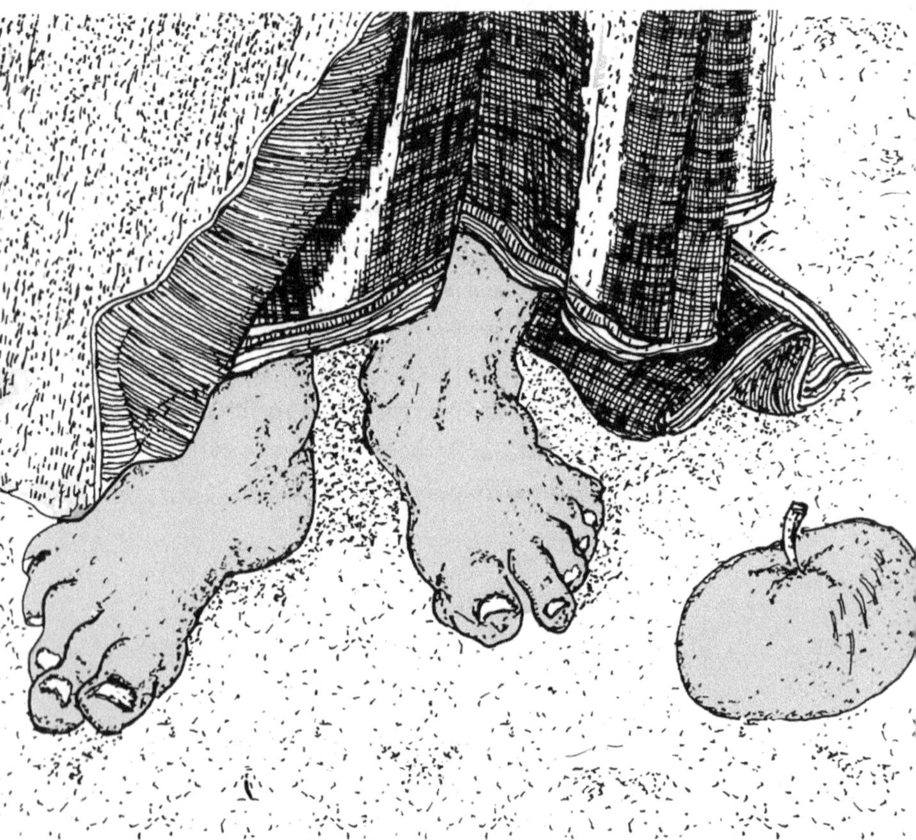

HALL OF FAME

These are the heroes — the Patrons and Pulp Literati whose monthly support helped bring you this issue. Please lift your glasses and give them a rousing cheer!

The Brewers
Robin McGillveray

The Landlords
Isabel Cushey
Dana Tye Rally
Adam Fout

The Innkeepers
Ada Maria Soto
Margot Landels
Ev Bishop
Susan Jackson
Kevin Harris
Gillian Gardiner
Richard Ohnemus

The Cicerones
Roger & Anne Anastasiou

The Bartenders
Alana Krider
Richard Gropp
Ron Graves
Kristen Mah
Victoria McAuley
Dave Wayne

Scott F Gray
Michelle Balfour
Abigail Bruce
Vernice Dietra Malik
Katriona Greenmoor
AD Bane
KT Wagner
Deepthi Atukorala
Margot Spronk
Margaret Elliott
Peter Halasz
Bjarne Hansen
Leny Wagner
Kain Stewart
Chris Olee
kc dyer
Kimberley Aslett
Jan Fagan
Brighton Hugg
Alexa Benzaid-Williams
Bryan Moose
Maureen Cooke
K Anastasiou
Mike Sylvester
Wichael Tellez
Katherine Derbyshire

Kerri Chamberlin
Rapscallion
Shannon Saunders
Megan Shaw
James Carlino

The Regulars
Marta Salek
Rina Piccolo
Jenny Blackford
Akemi Art
BC
Meredith Frazier
Catherine Levinson
Vera
Charity Tahmaseb
Marilyn Holt
Barbara Pengelly
David Perlmutter
Steve Mashburn
Christa Walker
Hannah McManus
Melissa Daniels
SR Harper

If you would like to join the ranks of these worthies, you can become a patron on Patreon at patreon.com/pulplit or join the Pulp Literati through our website at pulpliterature.com/join-pulp-literati/.

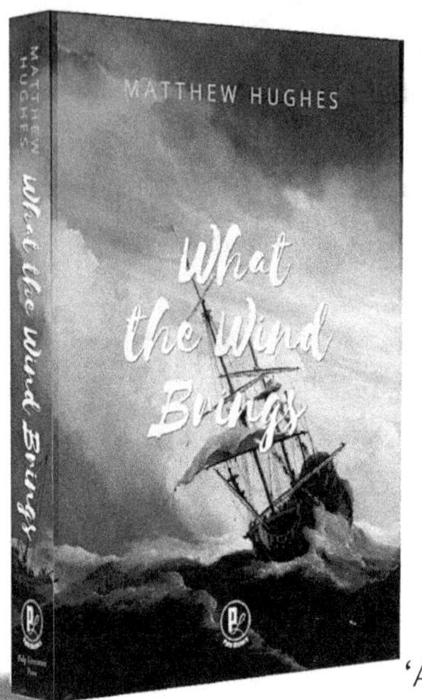

Out of the fires of a Caribbean slave revolt, shipwrecked on the jungle coast of 16th-century Ecuador, an educated slave, a shaman, and a monk hunted by the Inquisition fight for freedom against the might of Imperial Spain.

Dive into an epic slipstream novel of intrigue and adventure from fantasy author Matthew Hughes, the writer George R.R. Martin calls 'criminally underrated,' and Robert J. Sawyer says is 'a towering talent.'

'A triumph!' - Cecelia Holland
'Sensational' - Candas Jane Dorsey

pulpliterature.com

Fantastic Fresh Fiction!

Room Magazine

2022 Contest Calendar

Creative Non-Fiction
1st Prize: $1000 + publication
2nd Prize: $250 + publication
April 1 - June 15

Poetry
1st Prize: $1000 + publication
2nd Prize: $250 + publication
June 15 - August 31

Short Forms
1st Prize: $500 + publication
(two awarded)
September 1 - November 15

Covert Art
1st Prize: $500 + publication
2nd Prize: $50 + publication
November 15 - January 15, 2023

ROOM

Making Space in Literature, Art & Feminism Since 1975

Entry Fee: $35 (for entrants residing in Canada), $45 (for entrants residing in USA), $55 (for entrants residing anywhere else). Entry includes a one-year subscription to *Room*. Additional entries $7. Visit roommagazine.com/contest.

Do you have a **story to tell?**
We can help!

Dreamers is dedicated to heartfelt writing. Visit our site for:

- Therapeutic Writing
- Poems & Stories
- Content Marketing
- Creative Nonfiction
- Writing Workshops
- Contests & Anthologies
- Residencies & Retreats
- ...and so much more!

www.DreamersWriting.com

DREAMERS
CREATIVE WRITING

GEIST
go to geist.com/subscribe
or call 1-888-GEIST-EH
GEIST
LOST CITY
Keep it weird.
Subscribe today!
FACT + FICTION · NORTH of AMERICA

onspec
the canadian magazine of the fantastic
Expect the unexpected.
www.onspec.ca

MARCH 2022
MYSTERY MAGAZINE
All Original Stories
ORNTELLÀDAR
BY A.L. SIRDIS
MARTIN HILL ORTIZ
JAZZ LAWLESS
DIANE A. HADAC
KYLE DECKER
JOHN M. FLOYD
MEHNAZ SAHIBZADA
JOSH TAYLOR
JOHN H. DROMEY
Try our
You-Solve-it
MYSTERY !

The Digest Enthusiast
Book Fifteen C
January 2022
Tom Brinkmann
Steve Carper
Peter Enfantino
Stephen Jones
Gary Lovisi
Anthony Perconti
Jack Seabrook
David A Sutton

MICHAEL
KAMAKANA
ADVENT
WE THOUGHT WE KNEW WHAT THEY WANTED
WE WERE WRONG

HELP WANTED ?

If you are a new writer, or a writer with a troublesome manuscript,
EVENT's **Reading Service for Writers**
may be just what you need.

Manuscripts will be edited by one of EVENT's editors and receive an assessment of 700-1000 words, focusing on such aspects of craft as voice, structure, rhythm and point of view.

eventmagazine.ca

MARKETPLACE

Books

Advent *by Michael Kamakana* • We thought we knew what the aliens wanted. Think again. • pulpliterature.com/advent

Allaigna's Song: Chorale *by JM Landels* • The long-awaited conclusion to the bestselling *Allaigna's Song* trilogy. • pulpliterature.com/allaignas-song

The Extra: A Monument Studios Mystery *by Mel Anastasiou* • Extra Frankie Ray gets her big break on the Silver Screen, until Murder steals the scene. • pulpliterature. com/the-extra

The Labours of Mrs Stella Ryman: Further Fairmount Mysteries *by Mel Anastasiou* • Trapped in a down-at-the-heels care home. You'd be cranky too. • pulpliterature.com/stella-ryman-and-the-fairmount-manor-mysteries

What the Wind Brings *by Matthew Hughes* • Winner of the 2020 Endeavour Award • pulpliterature.com/product-category/novels/matthew-hughes

The Writer's Boon Companion *by Mel Anastasiou* • Thirty Days Towards an Extraordinary Volume • pulpliterature.com/subscribe/the-bookstore

Bookstores

Russell Books • 100-747 Fort St, Victoria, BC • russellbooks.com

Western Sky Books • 2132-2850 Shaughnessy St, Port Coquitlam, BC V3C 6K5 • 604-461-5602 • store.westernskybooks.com

White Dwarf / Dead Write Books • 3715 10th Ave W, Vancouver, BC V6R 2G5 • 604-228-8223 • whitedwarf@deadwrite.com

Conferences & Events

Word on the Lake • May 2023 • Salmon Arm, BC • wordonthelakewritersfestival.com

When Words Collide • August 4–6, 2023 • Calgary, AB • whenwordscollide.org

Wine Country Writers' Festival • Sep 2023 • winecountrywriters-festival.ca

Surrey International Writers' Conference October 2023 • siwc.ca

Printing & Publishing

First Choice Books/Victoria Bindery Book printing & binding • graphic design • eBooks • marketing materials • 1-800-957-0561 • firstchoicebooks.ca

Magazines

Amazing Stories · Back in print! amazingstories.com

The Digest Enthusiast · Digests past & present plus new genre fiction larquepress.com

EVENT Magazine · Poetry & prose eventmagazine.ca

Geist Ideas + Culture · Made in Canada geist.com

Mystery Magazine · The cutting edge of short mystery fiction www.mysteryweekly.com

Neo-opsis · Canadian magazine of science fiction based in Victoria, BC · neo-opsis.ca

OnSpec · The Canadian magazine of the fantastic · onspecmag.wordpress.com

Polar Borealis · Paying market for new Canadian SF&F writers & artists · polarborealis.ca

Room Magazine · Literature, Art & Feminism since 1975 · roommagazine.com

Writing Resources

Dreamers Creative Writing · Workshops, residencies, contests & more! · www. dreamerswriting.com

Quit the Day Job · A school for writers from Pulp Literature Press pulpliterature.com/quit-the-day-job

The Writers' Lodge on Bowen Island The Muse retreats for writers · pulpliterature.com/calendar-of-events/retreats/

A MONUMENT STUDIOS MYSTERY
THE EXTRA
MEL ANASTASIOU

CONTESTS

Pulp Literature runs four annual contests for poetry, flash fiction, and short stories. For contest guidelines, prizes, and entry fees, see pulpliterature.com/contests.

The Bumblebee Flash Fiction Contest
Contest opens: 1 January 2023
Deadline: 15 February 2023
Winner notified: 15 March 2023
Winner published: Issue 39, Summer 2023
Prize: $300

The Magpie Award for Poetry
Contest opens: 1 March 2023
Deadline: 15 April 2023
Winner notified: 15 May 2023
Winner published: Issue 40, Autumn 2023
Prize: $500

The Hummingbird Flash Fiction Prize
Contest opens: 1 May 2023
Deadline: 15 June 2023
Winner notified: 15 July 2022
Winner published: Issue 41, Winter 2024
Prize: $300

$\mathcal{B}$ecome a Patron of Pulp Literature

By supporting *Pulp Literature* on Patreon with $2 or more per month, you will be laying the foundation for a secure future for the magazine, as well as ensuring that you never miss an issue! Your subscription includes four big issues of short stories, novellas, poetry, comics, and novel excerpts, delivered to your door or electronic mailbox each year. **Find us at patreon.com/pulplit**

If you prefer to subscribe through our website, go to pulpliterature. com/subscribe.

Or you can send a cheque with the form below to
Subscriptions, Pulp Literature Press, 21955 16 Ave, Langley BC, V2Z 1K5, Canada

Don't miss an issue

- ❏   **Send me 2 years (8 issues) at the special rate of $90** (save $30)*
- ❏   **Send me 1 year (4 issues) for $50** (save $10)*
- ❏   **Send me 2 years of digital issues for $30** (save $9.92)
- ❏   **Send me 1 year of digital issues for $17.50** (save $2.47)

Name: ____

Address: ____

City: _________________________________ Prov. / State: _________

Postal code: _______________ Country:_____________________

Email: ____

❏	Payment enclosed	Make cheques payable in Canadian funds to Pulp Literatu
❏	Bill me	Press. Include email address for digital editions and Payp
❏	New	billing, or subscribe at www.pulpliterature.com.
❏	Renewal	*for postage outside Canada add $20 per year in North America $36 per year overseas.